I0590731

TALES FROM THE ORICERAN UNIVERSE

TALES FROM THE ORICERAN UNIVERSE

VOLUME 1

MICHAEL ANDERLE   TRACEY BYRNES   LISA FRETT

TR CAMERON   TIM BISCHOFF   KAT N SNOW

MANDI F   LUCINDA PEBRE   CRAIG LEWIS

DISRUPTIVE IMAGINATION

LMBPN Publishing
PMB 196, 2540 South Maryland Pkwy
Las Vegas, NV 89109

First US edition, January 2019

TALES FROM THE ORICERAN
UNIVERSE TEAM

Thank you to the following JIT Readers

Angel LaVey
Micky Cocker
James Caplan
Daniel Weigert
Misty Roa
Diane L. Smith
Chrisa Changala
Jeff Eaton

If we missed anyone, please let us know!

Editor Lynne Stiegler

INTRODUCTION

Road Trip!

What's better than stuffing Correk into the old green Mustang and grabbing the necessary snacks? (No eating them till we're out of the city limits... Leira rules) It's eight new stories packed with new adventures from Fans like you!

The Oriceran Universe is expanding and we're taking this show on the road. Hang on, I'll grab my mask and cape, just in case there's trouble.

We put out the word we were looking for new adventures and the Fans answered the call!

22 submissions, over 500 votes, and too many great stories to have just one volume of stories. That's right, **Volume 2** is already selected and will be out in March/April of this year!

There are 8 stories in this first volume. Five of the authors appeared in the Kurtherian Fans Write for the Fans anthologies, and there are three *new* voices joining the family. Some of the stories like **Trapped** are set back before humans knew Oriceran existed; the good-ol-days with just me and Leira (and Voodoo Donuts, Cheetos, Dr Pepper). Has anyone seen Hagan?

Some are set in the more cut-throat world of bounties and bounty hunters 20 years later ... I think Jed in **Black Magic Mafia** would get on great with Brownstone... Keepin' it simple.

There's even a story about my furry cousins back on Oriceran - shout out to my friends in **Troll Tales**! Someone tell Mom I'll be home for the Two Moons Dance.

Inspired to get involved?

Join us on Facebook at

https://www.facebook.com/groups/OriceranFansWrite

or join our sister group at

https://www.facebook.com/groups/TKGFansWrite

And don't forget to follow yours truly at https://www.facebook.com/OriceranTroll

Happy reading!

Yumfuck Tiberius Troll

TRAPPED

BY LUCINDA PEBRE

Being born into crime has its difficulties. In order to save her brother and herself, Stacey must enter a hotel belonging to her family's main competitor.

Stacey is a thief, but this job is different—the stakes are higher. She is forced to steal in exchange for her brother's life. When she finds an injured wolf, she discovers there's more in the universe than she has ever known, but now she has to choose whether to risk all or let the wolf die.

Jason will sacrifice everything, even himself, for his Pack. All humans lie and cheat, which is why he's aware of the dangers when he knowingly walks into their trap. What he didn't expect was to meet a woman who would selflessly risk herself to save him.

A growing attraction between the two threatens their lives. Trust can mean the difference between life and death in a world full of deceit and lies. Will they have the courage to trust each other?

DEDICATION

For mum, who would have loved this.

CHAPTER ONE

Death holds no fear for a warrior—unless he is chained to the wall of a cheap hotel room, waiting for Death to bring along his best friend Torture.

There was only one reason Jason was still alive: he'd managed to remain in human form, which wasn't what they wanted. No, they needed to see the animal to justify murder. At least, that's what he thought, although they weren't a cerebral lot, so perhaps it was something else.

Ordinary chains might not have held him, but there was something special about the metal coiled around his body. For one, it glowed with a greenish light and was slowly leaching his energy. He'd heard of a talisman that had the power to hold a shifter but had never encountered one.

He groaned. The whole situation was way too embarrassing, talisman or not. It might be better to let them kill him, because if he survived, he was never going to live this down.

He should have known from the beginning that it was a trap, but he'd been eager to have a solution to the problem that had been plaguing the Pack for years. That wasn't an excuse for forgetting one of the fundamental rules: *never trust a fucking human.*

Jason's head dropped toward his chest. It had been a stupid idea to come alone; it had been true arrogance. Tyler had argued against it, but since Jason, as Alpha, made the rules and Tyler only enforced them, there'd been no contest.

Both arms and legs were encased in a ridiculous number of chains. They clattered when Jason stirred, and the greenish glow they emitted nauseated him. He presumed any significant effort would alert a guard outside the door. He should be flattered that they thought he was that strong. In reality, it hurt too much to move. The reek of burnt flesh was enough to make him pass out, and the drain on his energy was just as bad as the pain.

They had not started torturing him yet, but with his superior hearing, he'd heard them discussing it; it wasn't something he wanted to stay around for. His mind played out various scenarios to get out of his predicament. Pain he could handle; it was mutilation that turned his stomach. As far as he could tell, they didn't want anything from him. Torture was probably their sport, and they'd get off on placing bets on how long he would last. If these chains hurt a little less and didn't weigh him down so much, he would beat himself around the head for being caught in the first place.

CHAPTER TWO

Stacey tucked her long blonde hair under a baseball cap. She should have it cut. The bloody stuff was too memorable and got her more attention than necessary. She closed her eyes, took a deep breath and thought of Aaron.

When they were kids, he'd always been the one leading the way into trouble. One of her first memories was of the time he'd broken into school for a copy of a test paper. There'd been no reason to take his baby sister along, but he'd called it "training". Naturally, they'd been caught, and since he was so much older, he'd taken the blame. That was why she had to do this now—for all the times he'd looked out for her.

From the furtive action behind reception, Security had been alerted as soon as she'd crossed the hotel's threshold. She sighed, there were times when a reputation could get in the way. Fortunately, on this occasion, that was precisely what she wanted.

Jez, Kemp's personal bodyguard, blocked her way. "Staaceey?" He drew her name out as if they were intimate. "Is this a personal visit?"

To anyone listening, the question would have seemed innocent enough, but she knew differently. She hadn't forgotten his last attempt to get her alone. Stacey was straightforward. She did not give mixed signals, and yet, despite consistently rejecting his advances, Jez persisted.

She saw him glance at the blue rucksack slung over her shoulder and wondered if he knew about her arrangement with his boss. What he couldn't know was that although her worldly belongings were in there, the item they wanted was not.

Tall and lean, she still only came to his shoulder. "Perhaps if you did something about that single eyebrow. Shave a track down the middle or something." His face turned a deep shade of red, but she didn't stop. "No, who am I kidding? Not a chance in hell."

Why couldn't she just keep her mouth shut? Perhaps it had something to do with the simmering rage inside. Stacey had no idea where it came from, only that it had been there forever, and she had to work hard to contain it in circumstances like these.

The two scars on Jez's right cheek became prominent against his skin. "I think we should discuss this in the back."

He was right. There were too many people watching, some of them criminals like her, searching for a job. The last thing she needed was this conversation getting back to her family. They'd think she'd lost her mind if she was caught dealing with Kemp.

Jez's shoulders were stiff as she followed him through the lobby. A woman with wispy hair and a heavily made-up face sat behind the check-in desk. Her eyes slid away from Stacey as if she were thinking, "See no evil, hear no evil, speak no evil." Shit, they were headed for the lifts.

Stacey thought she might have gone too far in pointing out his monobrow. "I have what Kemp wants." Not on her, but it was worth a try.

"Shame you had to get mouthy. I don't put up with mouthy bitches, whatever Kemp says."

She had to jog to keep up with his long strides. "That's part of my charm." There was no way she was going to be overly nice to this creep.

The gold doors of the lift opened with a jerk, and she stared dubiously inside. "Can't we take the stairs?"

"Up three floors? I don't think so." He grinned, displaying a missing right incisor. "You scared?"

Well, yes, but she would be damned before she'd show it. With a deep breath, she stepped into the small metal box and was immediately surrounded by mirrors. All four were broken. At the sight of her wide eyes displayed by multiple shards, she had the urge to giggle hysterically. Then Jez stepped inside and reality caught up with her.

The space shrank, and for a moment, Stacey could have believed that she'd entered the world of Alice in Wonderland. She became conscious of her heart thudding against her ribcage and had to concentrate to keep her breath even. Instead of coming up with a strategy to get her out of the situation, her brain chose to consider scenarios where she had managed to not get into the lift. A small knife dropped from her sleeve into her palm. It wouldn't be enough, but she'd fight.

Jez's face slowly morphed into a crazy grin. "I think we should discuss your attitude." His hand shot out to slap the red emergency button and the lift shuddered to a stop. Like she couldn't have guessed that was going to happen. "There might be a way for you to make it up to me."

If an opponent is a threat either due to skill or size, it's imperative that you strike first. Aaron had drilled that into her until she couldn't get it out of her head. The trouble was, that applied on the street where she could stab an enemy and run, not a confined space where she couldn't get away. And that was without the added complication of what Kemp would do if by some miracle she managed to kill Jez.

He reached out slowly, and she refused to back away. It would be a pointless exercise with the wall one step behind her. He flicked off her hat, which landed on the floor, where it would stay. She wouldn't bend down to retrieve it and make herself even more vulnerable.

Blonde hair tumbled down Stacey's back, warming her neck and ears. She held rigid, knowing that even a hint of fear would escalate the situation. She hadn't survived growing up with six brothers without learning a thing or two.

He leaned closer. "That's better. You shouldn't hide such beauty."

It took her a precious second to understand that he wasn't being sarcastic. He was serious, and that was not good. He started to step into her space, so they would be toe to toe.

Stacey's arm shot towards his head. The knife slashed skin above his eyes, and for a tense moment, nothing happened.

"Bitch!" His hand went up. "What did you do?"

She knew from the multiple stab wounds she'd had in the past that there would be a stinging sensation but little else. A line of blood appeared, slowly at first, then falling in a curtain into his eyes. Jez hit the emergency button, releasing the lift, with one big hand while the other covered his forehead. The wound wasn't deep and wouldn't hurt much now, but that hadn't been her intention. The appearance of the blood had had the desired effect of making him panic.

Stacey tried not to bask in the satisfaction of out-maneuvering an opponent. She wasn't out of danger, though; she had yet to face Kemp. He would be a much more significant challenge.

CHAPTER THREE

Jason heard a commotion outside the door, but the accumulative effect of the magic had taken its toll. He struggled to lift his head from his paws and focus. This must have been what they intended all along: leave him here to die. Yet, even knowing that, he didn't have the strength to do anything about it.

There was a male voice directly outside. "She needs to learn manners. Put her in with the wolf."

The part of his brain that still cared tried to work out what it meant and whether there might be an opportunity. He didn't want to die, although he was less concerned about that than he had been an hour ago.

There was a scuffle. "Careful, she's got a knife." A boot hit the bottom of the door. "Fuck." Something struck the wall.

A female voice said, "I have what Kemp wants. Tell him—"

The door opened halfway and a woman was thrust into the room. As she fell, she snatched a backpack from the hand that shoved her in. She landed on her ass but was up immediately, launching herself at the closed door. Blonde hair covered her shoulders and went halfway down her back.

Jason liked long hair.

The sound of three men laughing and congratulating each other came from the corridor outside, stirring something in Jason for a few seconds. He could only see her face in profile as he waited for her to bang on the door and shout to be let out.

She didn't. With hands bunched into fists, she took a deep breath and scowled at the door. "Glad I could provide a fucking bonding opportunity."

Jason chuckled, which came out as a whine. His throat was raw from the burning chain wrapped around his neck. It wouldn't be long before he'd lose consciousness.

The woman swung to face him. At first, he only registered big blue eyes, but as she cautiously approached him, he saw that she had delicate features and was pretty.

She stared at him like he might tear the chains out of the wall and attack. He'd tried that earlier; it hadn't worked. That was when he'd been stronger, which meant there was no chance of it now. In fact, he didn't think he had long left. He'd been wrong about the torture. It must have been their plan to kill him all along. There was little risk to them.

The woman was talking, and her soft voice had a lilt he rather liked. "Nice wolfie." She crouched slowly, trying not to frighten him. "What have they done to you with that heavy chain?"

She stayed out of reach, studying him. Sensible woman. Then, in an involuntary movement, she reached toward him.

Recognizing what she was doing, she snatched her hand back. "You poor thing. I can't leave you like this with all those chains hurting you."

Despite the state his body was in, Jason saw his chance. His tail thumped against the floor. It was a weak, half-hearted movement, but that wasn't surprising considering how he was feeling.

Fortunately, it was enough for the woman to move closer. He could hear her heart pounding, and sweat gleamed on her forehead. She smelled of fear, but that didn't stop her from coming forward.

"Nice wolfie." She closed the distance, touching his fur. Jason used his last bit of energy to shove his muzzle into her hand. His tongue lapped her salty skin, but instead of backing away, she froze. Then she reached to smooth the fur at the side of his face.

She smiled. "So soft."

He thought the woman's skin was soft, as well as delicate and feminine. If it hadn't been for the pain, he would have closed his eyes and enjoyed the attention.

Part of his brain wondered when he'd shifted into wolf form. He couldn't remember. At some point, he must have lost control and reverted to his animal state. It dawned on him how vulnerable his people would be with him gone. He whined.

"It's okay, baby."

The woman's voice soothed the part of him wanting to freak out. It occurred to him that she must think he was a normal wolf; she might not even know about shifters.

She rooted in her backpack and then used both hands to probe the area around the chain. There was an object in her hand that he couldn't see.

A stab of pain caused him to pull back. He whined again.

"It's going to be okay; I almost have it. You'll feel better if I can just get this off."

She was trying to remove the chain! He put his head in her lap, causing her to fall backward with a shriek. Perhaps that had been a bit sudden. He had forgotten how he must appear to her, although she had to be crazy in the first place to be petting a wolf as if he were a poodle.

When he stayed still, she resumed her work. Pain flared. The skin felt as if it blistered whenever the chain moved to a new patch of fur.

There was a small click, and the chain slackened. Relief was immediate. The woman paused and started to unwind the chain slowly, trying not to hurt him.

Jason wanted to race around and roll until it came free, but he made himself stay in the one spot. Although it seemed to be taking forever, he knew this was the fastest and safest way to remove the chain.

Jason's ears flicked towards the door. Someone was coming; they didn't have much time.

The woman continued her slow movements, oblivious to the danger. He wanted to tell her to hurry but could only whine. This was too frustrating.

A male voice came from the other side of the door. "Tell me you at least searched her."

"There wasn't time, and she snatched the bag."

"So, you don't even know if she has the artifact with her. Come on, she's a Bailey, they're as slippery as fuck."

There was the sound of a key being inserted into the lock and turned.

The woman's head came up. "Shit."

Jason stood, the rest of the chain slipping from his neck in a final flash of pain. His power didn't return, but adrenaline started coursing through his body, giving him strength.

The door started to open. Jason surged towards it, hitting the center and slamming it closed.

There was a rattle as the key turned. Footsteps hurried away, the two men whispering to each other.

"Silly boy." The woman had both hands on her hips and was glaring at the door.

Jason shook his body. It felt good. The pain in his neck had faded to a dull ache. He extended both front paws and arched his back in a satisfying stretch.

"Look, Wolfie, if we are going to get out of here, you need to listen. No more scaring the bad men away."

Jason stalked towards her, vaguely aware of the intimidating sight he presented. His furry shoulders came up to her stomach and his head to her chest, and in this form, he was about three times her weight. The way she spoke suggested that she knew what he was, but he doubted it. The fear he'd seen earlier was gone.

She didn't retreat as he moved closer. "My God, you're a big boy, aren't you?"

He'd been right in the first place; she was crazy. Why did that make him happy?

CHAPTER FOUR

Stacey knew it was stupid to get in the way of any wild animal with sharp teeth, and this one was so big, it had to be a male. For the moment, she was annoyed that he had scared off those two idiots. They could be out of here by now. She didn't have time for drama, although she was glad she'd saved the wolf.

Kemp would want to talk to her; she had something he wanted badly. That didn't matter if he didn't know she was here, though. Stacey had no choice; she had to find another way out. She glanced at her watch. Two hours and forty-five minutes until her brother was dead—unless she got there first.

There was no time to wait for the boss to find out she was here. If she was going to find Aaron, she had to act now.

It hadn't escaped her notice that if she hadn't upset Jez, she wouldn't have ended up trapped with His Furriness in the first place. That was beside the point. She didn't know anything about wolves, and this one had been hurt. His body was covered in burns, and those chains had been way too heavy for the animal.

The wolf growled low in his throat. By God, he was huge. He really was a beautiful animal, with a black and grey coat that gleamed enough to make a shampoo model envious. Distinctive markings across his face made it appear as if he wore a mask, and three of those adorable paws looked as if they'd been dipped in white paint. She would be able to identify him anywhere.

Hot breath warmed her bare arm as she studied the way his snout wrinkled when he was trying to be scary. Intellectually, she knew she should be afraid. He was a wild animal, and for all she knew, he had been chained in here to stop him from eating anyone.

The fearlessness that overcame her from time to time was her parents' fault, God rest their souls. They had indulged her far too much, teaching her that the world was safe and nothing could hurt her. Since their death, she'd had plenty of experiences that demonstrated the dangers out there. Nevertheless, confidence was still her go-to-position in life. Anyway, this wolf's eyes were too soft to convince her that he was mean.

"You don't have to thank me right now." She gestured to the pile of chains on the floor. "Buy me sushi at Urasawa and we'll call it even."

She laughed at her own joke, but the wolf stopped the low growling and sat back on his haunches. He tilted his head to one side slightly as if he didn't understand. Nothing new there. She was a mystery to most men; why not wolves as well?

"We need to get out of here, wolfie."

In answer, his body started to contort. Limbs lengthened, and his torso elongated.

Stacey didn't know what was happening. The fearlessness had left her; she was now staring at some sort of freak show with her heart thundering and her bladder threatening to abandon control.

Mesmerizing, she could not tear her eyes away. His body was reshaping into a human form—a very *male* human form. OK, so she had been right about that. She stared at the muscular thighs and the chest with its light dusting of hair. The man-wolf rose in front of her.

Oh, Lordy. One large gloriously naked male stood a couple of feet away. Wow, Wolfie was something. Big, and surprisingly not too hairy. Her eyes didn't know where to rest.

She tore her gaze away and went to look out the window. Perhaps if she ignored what she'd seen, she wouldn't go mad.

They were only on the third floor—not that it wasn't high enough for a fall to result in serious injury, but surely it'd be possible to climb down from this height. Except the double-glazed window was a sealed unit, and there was no convenient ledge to walk along. It might be possible to break the window, but it would make a lot of noise.

Heat radiated up her back and she swung round, palming a knife. They hadn't searched her very well before throwing her in here. She had more knives than they'd had time to find.

There really *was* a naked man in the room. She hadn't imagined it, and couldn't ignore it. No big deal; he must be a were-wolf. Did that mean he would want to eat her? If the books about vampires and werewolves were anything to go by, it could go either way. At least it explained the chains; although they didn't look like silver, there was a greenish tinge to them.

A mini fridge was across the room. There was probably food in there that would taste better than a human. He frowned and followed her gaze.

"I was thinking you must be hungry." She managed to get the words past a tongue that had tripled in size.

He grinned and strolled over to the fridge, giving her a view of his perfect ass. She watched as the muscles stretched and flexed, wondering if he would mind—

No. She had more important things to do, like find her brother. She gestured towards the bedroom. "There might be something in there you could wear."

It was only now that she noticed the ripped clothes scattered across the floor. She'd seen them when she came in, but thought they'd been left as bedding for the wolf. That didn't seem very likely now. They must be his clothes—the ones that hadn't survived transformation into a wolf.

Stacey tried not to look at his ass as he walked into the bedroom. Halfway there, he glanced over his shoulder and gave her a knowing wink.

Shaking her head, she tried to get her mind back on track. She supposed they were lucky to be trapped in a luxury room as opposed to one of the budget ones. There must be a way out.

CHAPTER FIVE

Jason found a whole closet full of clothes. Apparently, someone was occupying this room. He wondered which bar they were hanging out at while torture and mayhem went on among their possessions.

Unfortunately, most of the clothes were too tight. Eventually, Jason found a pair of sweat pants, which while they didn't leave much to the imagination, covered what was necessary. That might be a problem for the mouthy female next door. He generally avoided humans, but she had a sexy vibe he found appealing, and she'd helped him before she knew what he was. Who knew how she was going to react now?

He pulled on a white t-shirt, which stretched across his chest and made him look like a serious bodybuilder. He grinned and wondered if Ms. Sexy would like it. The shoes were too small, but his running shoes usually survived a shift. They would be somewhere in the other room.

He left the bedroom, noting with satisfaction that the woman's eyes widened and her breath hitched on his return. He should not care if she found him attractive, but he rather liked it.

He smiled to complete the effect. "Is this less distracting?"

She blinked rapidly. "Yeah, right. Great. Can you use your superpowers to get us out of here?"

Unbelievable! He'd never met anyone like her. The woman had just found out that shifters were real and rather than been awed into silence, she demanded that he magic them out of trouble.

Perhaps she mistook his silence for lack of understanding, because she said, "I know you're a werewolf and all, but I don't have much time. It'd be really cool if you had other powers."

He raised an eyebrow. "I'm a shifter."

"Same thing. Do you—" She frowned. "*Do* you have any powers?"

"I'm a shifter, not a bloody elf."

"Oh." She deflated, then immediately brightened. "There are elves?"

"Forget it. I'm Jason. Who are those people?" He gestured toward the door.

"Stacey, and you don't know?" There was a distinct note of disbelief in her voice.

He wasn't sure why he felt the need to justify himself. "I only know what they told me. They have something I need." He grinned. "You don't *look* ditzy."

"Do you think you're the first one to comment on my name?"

She rolled her eyes as she went to examine the hotel door. "You must be desperate." He was, but had no intention of discussing the details with a human. "I mean, some stranger offers you something in exchange for nothing, and you happily show up and let them drape you in chains."

"It wasn't for nothing," he mumbled. "Besides, they tricked me. What about you?"

She paused, considering how much to say. "I can't think of any reason not to tell you."

"Generous."

Her smile was there and gone within a second, but for a

21

moment Jason had the sense that he'd seen the true Stacey. "I'm looking for my brother. Kemp, the guy who owns this place, offered information if I did something." She shook her head. "No, not that sort of something."

He realized he was glowering and pulled himself together. "What then?"

She mumbled something even his sensitive hearing didn't catch. "Never mind. The point is, there's a deadline. I only have," she glanced at her watch, "another two hours and thirty-two minutes to find him."

It occurred to Jason that he was on a bit of a deadline himself. Tyler wouldn't sit at home for long. He was likely to do something drastic if Jason didn't turn up soon, no matter what orders he'd left; that was the downside of encouraging people to think for themselves. He went over to the window, studying the thick glass and heavy frame.

Her voice came from close behind. "I don't think we can get out that way."

She was quiet for a human. They usually stumbled around, banging into things. He half-turned, wanting to keep her in sight. It was disconcerting going from wolf-vision to human. The narrowing of perspective always felt wrong for hours afterward.

She gestured at the ceiling "I'm thinking we might be able to knock a hole in the ceiling. I mean, it's only plasterboard."

"Hotels are made of concrete."

"We're on the top floor."

He narrowed his eyes; she was right. "Umm, it's possible." He went into the other room and stood on the bed where he could easily reach the ceiling. A hollow tap confirmed it. "This will be noisy."

She handed him a lamp. "Hold on. I'll put the TV on loud."

"That might draw their attention."

"It's a risk," she acknowledged.

He waited, hefting the lamp, which was made out of metal. It should be sturdy enough for the job. It occurred to him that Stacey was smart as well as brave and pretty.

The blare of a TV came from the next room. Not wanting to waste any time, Jason immediately started hitting the ceiling. Debris rained down, and he closed his eyes to protect them from the powdery dust.

It was easy once he'd pushed through into the cavity above. He got both hands into the hole and pulled the plasterboard out until the gap was big enough. Dust filled the air covering his white t-shirt in streaks of black.

"You've made quite a mess." She stood at the end of the bed with her hands on her hips.

Although the hole was big enough, he realized there wasn't anything to grab to pull himself up. The edges wouldn't hold much weight.

He turned his attention to Stacey. There was nothing for it; he would have to trust the human. This must be the universe's way of getting revenge for all the times he'd gotten away with driving too fast and clever stunts like jumping off high cliffs into the sea.

Jason peered into the hole. "Come on, I'll hoist you up."

From the doorway, a man shouted, "Stop!"

The TV continued to blast from the other room, which must have been why Jason hadn't heard him come in.

CHAPTER SIX

Stacey swung around to find Kemp and Jez a few steps away. Their faces were frozen in shocked surprise, and neither appeared to have a weapon.

She looked over her shoulder at Jason and mouthed, "Go!" They wouldn't hurt her. Well not immediately; not while she had something Kemp wanted.

Jason hesitated for a heartbeat, then, using the bed as a springboard, jumped. His head and upper body vanished. There must have been something for him to grab up there because the rest of his body and legs quickly disappeared through the hole.

Jez yelled something incoherent and raced forward, pushing Stacey out of the way. She barely caught herself on the wall. In his attempt to follow, Jez jumped and grabbed the edges of the plasterboard, which broke off in his hands. He landed on the bed with more of the ceiling on top of him.

Stacey couldn't hold back her laugh. She put both hands over her mouth and closed her eyes to block out the sight of Jez on the hotel bedspread coated in white dust and dirty insulation.

Kemp glared at her. "What exactly were you doing with that creature?"

She stopped laughing. She still had to find her brother, and she couldn't do it locked up. "We were trying to get out of this crappy hotel room." Stacey tried to rein in her temper before she said something that got her into more trouble. Lowering her voice, she continued, "You know I don't have much time left. I couldn't waste it lounging in here after he locked me in." She pointed at Jez, just in case Kemp didn't know what had happened.

"Do you have the ring?"

"Not with me. I'm not stupid enough to walk in here where you could just take it."

Instead of the expected annoyance, Kemp nodded. "Good. Let's go."

"You go. I don't have time for a trip."

"You haven't got a choice." He gave her a sinister smile she bet would work well on Halloween.

Why did she have the feeling that he wasn't talking about going to fetch the artifact? That would at least make sense. It was a small comfort that they would never find it without her. The one thing every thief knew was how to protect their own valuables, or in this case, someone else's. Stacey had no intention of keeping the ring; it wasn't to her taste. She didn't like the way it felt almost slimy. If she wasn't careful, her imagination could get carried away.

They got into the elevator again. Jesus, it was only three floors. Just how unfit *were* they? Stacey's body automatically tensed when she stepped inside, but she wasn't as worried with Kemp present. Jez was the one she had to watch, since he kept darting vicious glares in her direction. She had no trouble returning them. Yes, it would be sensible to cultivate people to her side, but she didn't have the time or inclination.

They traveled in silence to the lobby, where Jez had a word with the woman at the desk. Probably organizing for someone to clean up the mess they'd left behind.

"Whose room was that?" Stacey asked, intent on making small talk to distract them from questioning her.

Kemp ignored her, his eyes lingering on staff passing through the lobby. They scurried past as if afraid that if they didn't move fast enough, he would pounce.

"Just making conversation," she muttered.

Once Jez joined them, they proceeded to the parking lot at the front. It was half-full of crappy vehicles, with the occasional mid-range car or truck. Stacey wasn't interested in who was there, but it was good practice to maintain awareness of her surroundings. That was why she scanned the parking lot. There was nothing out of place, so why did she feel as if someone were watching her?

CHAPTER SEVEN

Jason threw the pen across the room, dissatisfied when it bounced off the wall without smashing into pieces. Placing both elbows on the desk, he rested his head in his hands.

What the hell was wrong with him? He couldn't concentrate, and he needed to. Every day that went by without a solution risked the health and wellbeing of the children and young people in the Pack. It should be a simple matter to get what they needed, but nobody had been able to help. And where the hell was Tyler?

After what had happened earlier with the humans... Jason pulled away from thinking about her, forcing his mind back to the matter at hand. He did not want to go to the Dark Elves. The last thing the Pack needed was to owe them anything. Who could trust that they would even deliver?

Tyler had been waiting at the rear entrance of the hotel when Jason made it out. Once Tyler had picked himself off the floor from laughing at the clothes Jason wore, he agreed to follow Kemp's car.

Jason told himself he would have gone back in for Stacey. Only because he owed her, not for any other reason. But then, they'd seen her come out with Kemp and Jez. Jason had wanted to be the one to follow them, but Tyler had insisted on going. It was unfortunate, but Jason had a reputation to repair.

He rubbed his chest. The decision to return without making sure she was safe had resulted in something akin to heartburn. Nevertheless, he was not going to think about her. Even her name conjured inappropriate images. There was too much to do and think about without getting mixed up with a human.

Tyler walked in without knocking, as usual, stopping to pick up the pen, iPhone with a broken screen, and journal cover. The rest of the book was under the chair.

Jason stood. "Where is she?"

"Outside a restaurant with the two she left with and a man who can only be her brother."

"She's okay, then? How did you know it was her brother?" It bothered Jason that the statement didn't make sense. Her brother was missing. It seemed unlikely those two would just take her there unless there was something in it for them.

"I never said she was okay, and the guy looked like her." Tyler leaned against the doorframe. "Are you interested in her?"

"Don't be an idiot." Jason pulled open a drawer and began rummaging, not sure what he was looking for. "She's human."

"So?"

"You know how I feel about humans—"

"Yeah, yeah, they're all weak and self-centered and the planet would be better off without them." Tyler came into the room and flopped into the chair opposite Jason. "Just admit you like her and give her a call. It isn't that hard."

Jason snapped, "She isn't interested, and I have no way of contacting her."

It would be a good idea to change that chair for something modern and uncomfortable. Wasn't that what they did in fast food places to get a quick turnover? People might leave him alone then.

Tyler threw back his head and laughed. "Believe me, she's

interested. Who wouldn't be? Besides, I can't put up with you brooding like this. You're no good to anybody. Do you want me to tell you where she is?"

"No, I want you to do your bloody job."

Still chucking, Tyler placed both hands on the desk to push up and meandered out of the office, singing, "*This thing called love, I just can't handle it. This thing called love, I must get 'round to it. I ain't ready. Crazy little thing called love.*"

Jason shook his head, scowling. There was nothing to be happy about. But perhaps he should just check that she was okay. Bloody hell, this was getting him nowhere.

"Tyler!" he bellowed. "Get your ass back in here."

CHAPTER EIGHT

Stacey sat in the shade of the wall, doing her best to stay out of the searing sun. Kemp and Jez had left when she'd refused to believe Aaron wasn't being coerced. She still wasn't convinced that they didn't have a sniper at his back or something. That was the only thing that would make sense, because the brother she'd been thinking of for the past two months wasn't the person who sat in front of her now.

Aaron was saying, "Everyone in the family has to face a test. This was uniquely yours. You needed to be motivated, Stacey. Motivated into carrying on family tradition rather than going to college to do social studies or whatever."

"Criminology, moron."

He laughed as if she hadn't just insulted him. "That's rich. Our little thief learning about crime." He shook his head. "The point is, your *job* is to contribute to this family. We take care of each other, and with me leading the way, we're going to be great." Removing the linen napkin from his knee, he smiled. "Do you have something for me?"

Perhaps he'd stopped his recitation because he sensed that she was close to smashing the plate of pasta in his face. Come to think of it, he'd always been single-minded and when he got an idea in his head; there was no reasoning with him. Did he know how annoying that could be? Then it dawned on her that he was asking about the ring he'd arranged for her to steal.

"I almost got caught stealing that damned thing. What do you want it for, anyway?"

"It's powerful. I need it."

Yesterday she would have scoffed at the idea that an object had power, but after meeting a wolfman, anything was possible.

He looked like a petulant child when she didn't immediately answer, but she wasn't sorry for him, not this time. "What about the wolf?"

Aaron pushed away his plate. "Did those idiots finish the job?"

Her eyes widened. "You meant to kill him?" Now that she thought about his condition when she'd been thrown into that room, they'd come close. "They almost did."

"Stacey, it isn't really a wolf —"

"No, *he* is a man." She pushed her chair back, making it vibrate on the concrete. "Why would you do that?"

"Lower your voice. People are looking." He glanced at the nearby tables. "We were contracted to take him out by some powerful...creatures. Apparently he causes a lot of trouble in the local area."

"So, you're a murderer now?"

He grimaced. "Werewolves aren't human, so they don't count. They are not natural."

"Shifters," she mumbled.

This wasn't getting them anywhere. It was like she didn't know the man sitting opposite. He had changed a lot in a short space of time, and she wondered how. What had happened to the boy who'd swum out to rescue a cat clinging to a branch? The kid who'd mowed the lawn for their neighbor when her arthritis got too bad?

"Who are you working for, Aaron?"

"Nobody. It was just a job. Once the wolf is dead, that's the end of it."

Stacey saw the motorbike pull up illegally at the edge of the main road. There was plenty of room for the traffic to flow around it, but it was a weird place to stop.

At first, she didn't pay too much attention. She had other things on her mind, not least making sense of this pile of shit. Then the biker revved the engine. She couldn't see his eyes, just a black helmet and yet she knew he was staring at her.

No, it *couldn't* be. Had he come to make sure she didn't tell anyone about him? She wouldn't, since she had no intention of being branded a nut job.

A quick look confirmed that Aaron hadn't noticed. Not wanting him to see—because it had to be Jason—she kept the bike in her peripheral vision. She didn't like how Jason made her feel. It was as if she needed something from him, but that girly shit was something to examine later when her entire future didn't hang in the balance.

She scowled. "I thought you were hurt or dead or a prisoner." The anger that had been simmering was now growing. It felt like a physical entity trying to get out. "How could you do that to me?"

Aaron's face hardened. "As the only girl, you've been spoiled for far too long. Not just by mom and dad, but by everyone. It's time you faced up to your responsibilities."

That was it. Aaron had always behaved like he was Mr. Special. For some reason, he thought being the eldest made him better.

She narrowed her eyes. "Let me get this straight: you want me to hand over the same ring you tricked me into stealing?" He opened his mouth to respond, but she continued, "Not that you risked yourself for, but used your *little sister* to get. Really?" She was laying it on thick, but the more she thought about it, the angrier she became. "You might be the eldest, but you are hardly qualified to take charge!"

When he opened his mouth to answer, she said, "Be very careful."

"Stacey, you have to see reason."

She stood, having known for a few minutes what she was going to do. Somehow Jason's presence made everything clear. There was no point trying to convince Aaron of anything. He was too far gone.

"Stacey, if you walk away, that's it. You will no longer be a part of this family."

She couldn't help glancing at the motorbike, needing to check that it was still there. The small plume of steam coming from the exhaust told her he was ready. If she concentrated, she could almost feel the engine throbbing in the center of her chest.

Turning her attention back to Aaron, she said, "But staying means living by your rules. Mom and dad would never have stopped me from going to college or having a life."

"Our parents were too soft on you. They allowed you to have ideas that should have been squashed as soon as they started."

Stacey had no doubt that Aaron was serious. He was the most stubborn person she'd ever met and if she walked away from him today, she would be leaving anyone who took his side. That meant it was likely she would never see her nieces and nephews again. While it hurt, she could end up a victim for the rest of her life if she stayed. He would destroy everything that made her who she was until she obeyed him without question.

Aaron was her brother; she didn't think he was evil, just misguided. But that didn't mean he wasn't dangerous. No, it was best not to start down that path. Aaron had tried to murder someone for gain, and she couldn't live with that.

As if he were able to read her thoughts, the biker's helmet turned in her direction. Despite the distance, she felt the unspoken question.

Jason belonged to a world into which she'd dipped a toe. He was unpredictable and dangerous, but also mysterious and exciting. She wanted more.

Stacey stepped back, her body already reaching out to the leather-clad shifter. "Let me ask you something: if you had to choose between the ring and me, which would it be?"

"I don't have to choose." He didn't understand that with those words, he'd given her his answer.

"Here." She unhooked the backpack containing her clothes and books from the chair and threw it at him.

She started towards the bike as the engine revved, louder than it should have been able to. When she swung towards it, she saw that it had left the road and was on the verge, heading her way. The back wheel spun on the soft grass, churning up mud and spraying clods of earth against a billboard. What was he doing?

Then she saw a black Jeep tearing across the parking lot to mount the curb. It was coming for her, and Kemp was behind the wheel. Jez was in the passenger seat with both hands braced on the dashboard. For a moment she struggled to take in the danger. Aaron wouldn't hurt her, would he?

Stacey ran, the thought of getting to the bike driving her. Part of her was tempted to stop and prove that her brother wouldn't kill or injure her, but when she threw a glance in Aaron's direction, he was busy digging through the backpack. He wasn't even interested in the outcome of the assault he must have initiated.

She almost returned to hit him over the head when she saw her well-worn *Kurtherian Gambit* novel fall to the floor. The bastard! There was no way he was getting that ring now.

Stacey stumbled on the uneven sidewalk but managed to right herself. The car was gaining speed. There was no way it would be able to stop in time, even if Kemp stamped on the brakes.

Both arms pumping, she sailed over a trash bag and ran like she'd never run before. The bike slowed, turning in front of her.

The roar of the Jeep's engine was growing louder. She didn't need to check to know it was too close.

With one hand on the biker's arm, she swung up behind him and hung on for dear life. They bounced onto the road, where he let out the throttle.

A pulse of familiar energy went through her, and she hugged Jason tight. The wind whipped at her hair. It was too noisy to speak, which was a shame because she had loads of questions.

Stacey couldn't resist swiveling to see what was happening behind them. The Jeep had stopped next to Aaron, who stood at the curb with her empty backpack dangling from one hand. She vowed that Aaron Bailey would never get the artifact.

Stacey had risked her life on a futile mission to save her brother and discovered the world was bigger than she thought. Now the future was wide open, and she had never been so scared in all her life—yet she had never felt so free.

AUTHOR NOTES

Thank you for reading *Trapped*. It is scary to put a piece of myself out there and then invite judgment, but it feels like a good way to grow my writing skills. If you'd like to read more, visit lucindapebre.com.

I don't know why some stories come out more easily than others, but this one was just waiting to be written. Not only that, nothing much changed during my editing process, which is rare for me. I usually find that I have to work hard on a story's structure once I have a first draft.

You can probably tell that *Trapped* is part of a larger story. Unfortunately, I don't know what will happen next; I never do until I write. The story goes where it wants, regardless of whether I have planned and plotted. If I try to force it, I end up staring at a blank page. That means unless I continue to write and expand this into a novella or novel, I won't know what happens to Stacey or Jason. Both characters now belong to the Oriceran world, and I cannot adequately express how wonderful it has been to be allowed to contribute to that ever-expanding universe, regardless of whether this story is published.

If anyone is thinking about having a go at writing a story, just do it. You won't regret accepting the awesome opportunity. It's been great fun, and everyone has been genuinely helpful and supportive. This is my second short story for LMBPN, and hopefully not my last.

Thank you, Martha Carr and Michael Anderle for creating such a special, safe place for readers and authors

Lucinda Pebre

WHITE MOUNTAINS MANIFESTATION

BY TRACEY BYRNES

Three teenagers. A hike in the White Mountains. And a moose…
What could possibly go wrong?
A lot…especially when ancient magic enters the mix.

For everyone who's encouraged me to set the magic free, then keep following wherever it leads. You rock.

CHAPTER ONE

What do you do when, sixteen years after you were born to human parents who've never shown an ounce of magical talent, you suddenly manifest the ability to create and manipulate ice?

In my case, the answer was, "Freak the hell out." As in, I damn near froze *myself* to death on a hot and humid-as-hell ninety-degree day because the more I lost my shit, the more dramatic and far-reaching the ice became. Good thing we were in an isolated meadow deep in the White Mountains National Forest when it happened, because it resulted in a fairly large meltdown.

I mean all the ice I created, of course. Although if I'm honest, I'm referring to my meltdown too. Don't judge.

Oh, wait. I should probably introduce myself before spilling the whole tale. My name is Sin. Or rather, that's my nickname—short for Sindratha—and the only name I'll answer to.

Contrary to what *some* people in town think, I don't live up—or is it down?—to my nickname. I'm generally very well behaved, even for a teenager. No drinking, no drugs, no wild parties, no cow-tipping or vandalizing property because I'm bored or think it's fun. I just don't like how pretentious my full name sounds, so

43

I shortened it and refused to answer to anything but "Sin" until it became second nature for everyone.

Okay. Back to the story.

My family and I live in the White Mountains region of New Hampshire. Think the Presidential Range—lots of national forests and state parks, Mount Washington, the Cog Railway, Story Land, and several well-known ski areas that also have summer-side activities like ziplining and canopy tours. The Conway Scenic Railroad also runs through here for part of its route.

There are tons of places to hike and stay in the area, everything from bare-bones "roll up in a tarp in the woods" to posh resorts where you can immerse yourself in luxury after a day spent hiking through God's country—or cruising around in your vehicle checking out the local artisans and attractions if you're not the outdoors type.

My friends Becks, who's my age, and Sam, who's a year older, were with me on a day-long hiking trip. We'd chosen one of the trails that started on the Saco River a couple miles from Willey House. Yeah, that's a historic landmark. Google it if you want to know more.

We'd parked Sam's old Toyota Corolla at the trailhead, grabbed our backpacks, and headed out in the dewy coolness of a mid-July early morning. We planned to hike to a meadow that was far enough off the trail that most tourists didn't realize it existed, although it was well-known to the locals and U.S. Forest Rangers. We wanted to relax and recharge while surrounded by the beauty of nature. Becks, a gifted amateur photographer, brought her Nikon DSLR camera along.

Since we'd all been drilled in wilderness safety from the time we were little kids, our families knew where we'd be hiking. We'd sent them the GPS coordinates of the trailhead where we'd parked, and planned to send them the coords for the meadow as well. It was worth an extra minute of caution to avoid becoming the next reason the U.S Forest Rangers and local volunteer SAR crews had to be sent out.

A couple of hours and a considerable increase in elevation into our hike, we turned off the main trail onto a faint game trail. If you weren't watching carefully, you'd miss the subtle indicators. We didn't precisely discourage tourists from finding the meadow...but we didn't encourage them, either.

About fifteen minutes after we'd turned onto the game trail, we broke through the trees and scrub brush that ringed the meadow. The grass was still dew-covered although it was drying in the sunlight. We walked quietly, our hiking boots making faint *shshing* sounds in the wet grass as we headed toward the widest part of the meadow.

By unspoken mutual agreement, we stopped on a slight knoll. It gave us great line-of-sight all around, which was ideal for Becks' longer-range photos. We texted the GPS coordinates to our parents, then unstrapped our rolled-up ground tarps from our backpacks. We spread the tarps on the grass before shrugging out of our packs and setting them down on the tarps as anchors. It wasn't windy at the moment, but that could change at any time.

I stretched, seeing Sam and Becks do the same before I closed my eyes and turned my face upward, enjoying the warmth of the sun against my skin. Finishing my stretch, I opened my eyes and folded down into a cross-legged position on my tarp. Sam sprawled out on his an arm's length away on my right. Becks had her camera in hand and was standing next to hers, which was down by Sam's and my feet, forming the base of a rough triangle. It was the best formation for us to talk and still keep an eye on our surroundings.

I looked in the direction Becks was focused on and caught a quick white flash through a small opening in the brush at the edge of the meadow just as I heard the camera's shutter clicking rapidly. A split second later I saw a deer leap past the opening and deeper into the trees. Becks lowered her camera and plopped down on her tarp.

"Did you get it?" I was curious, since it had been well-hidden before it moved, then gone before you could even say, "Deer!"

Becks shook her head. "I doubt it. I mean, I probably caught *something*, but I doubt it's clear. Suckers are just too damn quick when they get startled like that. The brush camouflaging it didn't help."

I chuckled. "Maybe next time one will oblige you by coming out into the meadow."

"That would be mighty nice of it," Becks replied straight-faced, knowing I was teasing while being serious about wanting that kind of opportunity for her.

Sam's laughter joined ours as Becks set her camera down close at hand and laid on her back to gaze at the blue sky.

We were quiet for a while, each absorbed in our thoughts and enjoying the peaceful setting. The only sounds were the whistling moans of the intermittent breeze that rippled the grass around us, the sporadic piercing calls of the birds flying overhead, our rhythmic breathing, and the occasional scuff of our clothes or shoes against a tarp.

Eventually Sam's deep baritone broke the quiet. "Penny for your thoughts, Sin."

I spoke lazily. "Not sure they're worth even that much, Sam. I wasn't really thinking of anything."

"No? I figured your mind was probably racing."

Although he spoke lightly, there was truth in his words. My mind usually *was* going ninety miles an hour in several different directions.

"Touché. But no, not right now."

"Well, carry on." His smile was evident in his voice. "Becks, how about you? Any thoughts worth a penny?"

"Not a one, Sam." Her amusement came through clearly in her

reply. "How about you? I mean, since you're asking…" Her unspoken implication was clear.

He laughed. "Guilty as charged. Want to go wading in the stream?"

Now that my attention was firmly back in the here-and-now, I realized the temperature had climbed and it was muggy as hell. My clothes stuck to me as I shifted and stood up.

"Sounds good to me." My voice was somewhat breathy since I was bent over rolling up my tarp when I replied. "Becks? You in?"

"You bet," came her quick response. "I feel like I'm in a steam room right now. That cold water will feel great."

CHAPTER TWO

I finished strapping my tarp to my backpack and swung the bag onto my shoulder. Becks and Sam did the same, then we headed toward the other end of the meadow at a steady pace. Becks snapped some pictures during our short trip. I had no idea how she kept the camera steady, but I'd seen some of the raw photos she'd captured during previous hikes and they were crystal-clear.

It took us about fifteen minutes to get to the stream, and by that time we were sodden with sweat. After dropping our packs on the grass near the bank, we took off our hiking boots and socks. We tucked the socks inside the boots and set them neatly beside our respective packs, ready to grab at a moment's notice.

Sam also stripped off his t-shirt before heading down a sandy washout to the clear water burbling over the streambed. The sun gleamed on his tanned, sweat-covered skin. Becks and I sighed wistfully, wishing we could ditch our shirts too, but although we always carried a towel apiece in our bags neither of us had packed a swimsuit.

A sudden yelp followed by a string of creative language had Becks and me doubled over laughing until we cried. Apparently, Sam had waded straight into the knee-deep water, discovering that it was still limb-numbingly cold in spite of the week-long heat wave we'd been in.

"Go ahead, laugh it up," he growled. "Payback will be sweet."

Becks and I traded mischievous smiles before walking down the washout into the water. The cold was a shock, but it didn't stop us as we flanked Sam and splashed him.

He yelped again, then retaliated. All of us were careful to keep the splashing minimal. Even though it was hot, it was too muggy for our clothes to dry if we got soaked. Wet clothes would mean chafed skin and an uncomfortable hike back; something we wanted to avoid.

We splashed around for a while, seeing who could send water flying the farthest and generally having fun. Eventually we grew tired and climbed some rocks protruding from the grassy bank, bypassing the washout to keep our feet as dirt-free as possible. All three of us grabbed our tarps, spread them on the grass, and laid down on them, using our packs as headrests.

I was in that semi-aware state where you're halfway between waking and sleeping when I heard the shutter on Becks' camera go off. I opened my eyes but stayed still, knowing that movement was likely to spook whatever creature she was photographing. The shutter sounds stopped and I heard her inhale before she spoke quietly, her voice tense and tightly controlled.

"Sin. Sam. Turn your heads slowly to the left."

I did as she asked and Sam did the same. Then I gulped, my attention riveted on the huge bull moose that was standing about fifty feet away, watching us as intently as we were watching it.

CHAPTER THREE

I don't know if you're familiar with moose, but when I say "huge," I'm referring to an adult bull moose that weighed somewhere around twelve hundred pounds and stood maybe six feet tall at the shoulder. Not his back or his head, his *shoulder*. This guy would make a full-size jacked-up pickup truck look small—and if it came to an altercation between the two, the moose would win.

As we watched—carefully, since animals often perceive focused attention as a threat—we tried to keep calm, although it wasn't working very well. Mr. Moose probably knew exactly how scared we were since moose have excellent senses of smell and hearing. Their vision isn't great; they're near-sighted critters with binocular vision, which means they need to be close to see things clearly, but something directly in front of them is in a quasi-blind spot if it's too close.

I'm not sure what started the chain of events, but the next thing I knew, Mr. Moose was pacing toward us, head and antlers starting to lower. The three of us kind of lost our heads. Wilderness-savvy or not, when something that big and unpredictable comes at you, "fight or flight" kicks in hard. Becks and Sam leaped to their feet and turned into world-class barefoot sprinters. I made it to my feet, my hand clutching my nana's old medallion—then froze.

It wasn't due to fright. My body shook with cold before getting so frigid I couldn't shake anymore. Ice crystals were rapidly building in layers on my shirt. I suspected that was happening all over my body, but I couldn't look. My attention was focused on Mr. Moose, who'd come even closer and was snorting at me.

I was screaming in my head, wanting to run. Wanting Mr. Moose to get the hell away from me. *Anything* to get out of this potentially deadly situation. Guess I should've been a bit more careful with my wishes, because the next thing I knew, everything around me was icing over. Not pretty sparkling frost, but true ice. The meadow, the stream, the trees, the rocks...and me. Even Mr. Moose was growing small icicles on his hairy hide.

My eyes widened, and my screams finally broke free. Bad move on my part, because they upset Mr. Moose even more. I'm pretty sure I saw my life flash before my eyes in that FML moment, then the most astonishing thing happened: a wave of ice built a thick barrier between us even as a layer covered my mouth and silenced my screaming.

Fraught moments passed as I imitated an ice-covered statue while waiting for Mr. Moose to leave. I couldn't move or speak; I couldn't even feel my body. I wondered if Mr. Moose would leave before I died of hypothermia.

A sudden *crack!* on the other side of the meadow drew Mr. Moose's attention and he swung his head around to look, then turned and started ambling in the direction of the noise. I had no idea what it was or why it so readily gained his attention, but I wasn't going to argue. I still had a huge dilemma to figure out.

CHAPTER FOUR

Becks and Sam moved warily back toward me, slipping and sliding as they crossed the ice-covered ground. They stopped a good distance away.

"Sin? What's going on?"

Sam snorted at Becks' question. "Seems pretty obvious, Becks. Magic."

I'd have laughed out loud if I could've since Sam's response was so close to the one running through my head.

"Ok, Sin, Mr. Moose is off on his next adventure. It's safe to let the ice melt. Can you calm down enough to do that?"

I rolled my eyes.

"Hey, now. I'm not a magic user, but I know some of the principles. Seriously, if you can calm your mind, your emotions will settle too. Once they do, the magic should fade."

Hmm. He had a point. Since *none* of this was under my conscious control, emotions had to be driving it—which meant I needed to calm the hell down before things turned dire. Or more dire than they already were, since I wasn't confident I could thaw myself before freezing to death.

Sam must've figured out some of what was going through my head.

"You can do this, Sin. Breathe with me. Focus on matching my breathing, nothing else. Inhale, two, three, four, five, six, seven, eight. Exhale, two, three, four, five, six, seven, eight."

He led me through that measured breathing for what seemed like hours, but in reality wasn't that long. As I settled into the rhythm, my mind and emotions quieted—and the ice covering my mouth melted. I nearly shouted for joy but caught myself just in time.

"That's it, Sin. Keep breathing, nice and even. You're doing great."

Buoyed by that sign of success, I stuck with the measured breathing but added a thought—a wish, really—timed to my exhalations. *I want to be warm.* I kept repeating it, willing something to happen.

The next thing I knew, ice cracked off me in some places while streams of water poured off others. As soon as the ice locking me in place released its grip, I collapsed to the ground, exhausted and shivering uncontrollably.

"Sin!" Becks yelled, her feet going every which way as she tried to race toward me. One part of my mind noted the hilarity of my normally-graceful friend flailing like a hapless contestant on Spike TV's *Most Extreme Elimination Challenge*, but I appreciated her attempt to reach me.

"Keep breathing, Sin. Whatever you're doing, it's working." Sam's deep voice washed over me as he resumed counting while slowly and carefully working his way toward me. Or rather, toward our backpacks, I realized as I saw him angle slightly to my left.

By now there were large puddles everywhere. Mist—or was it fog? I couldn't remember the difference—was rising around us as melting ice met the hot, humid air. It was difficult to see the shaking hand I managed to raise in front of my face, let alone Becks or Sam.

"You're doing great, Sin."

Sam's voice was my anchor as I kept breathing and wishing…*willing* the ice to melt faster so I could be warm again.

"Becks, you'll need to carry your pack and Sin's plus your hiking boots until we get to drier ground. I'll get my pack, boots, and Sin, once she's finished de-icing. She won't be able to walk while she's shaking like that." There was a note of humor in his voice, even though he was completely serious.

"Hardy-har-har," I managed to get out through chattering teeth.

When a sudden breeze shredded the fog, I saw that the ice in the meadow and trees had melted, creating a large water-logged area. We were in for a wet slog out, no matter which way we went.

The sound of splashing water drew my attention. When I glanced over at the stream, I was shocked to see it running considerably lower than when we'd played in it earlier. The splashing was due to several mini-streams now draining into it from the over-saturated ground.

"Yep, that's due to your ice-capades. I suspect you also pulled water from the natural pool a little further upstream. Otherwise this part would be dry." Sam spoke easily, although I knew he was still concerned.

Becks spoke up several minutes later. "Looks like you're pretty well de-iced now. So's the ground in your immediate vicinity, as far as I can tell."

Sam assessed me. "Yep, she's right. Ready to get out of this waterpark?"

I snorted, although it was hard to tell given my chattering teeth. "Only you, Sam," I managed to get out.

He flashed a mischievous grin while shrugging into his pack.

"Someone's gotta keep you entertained and calm. Might as well be me."

Becks laughed as Sam bent down and scooped me up.

"This isn't going to be comfortable, Sin, but it's the least taxing way to carry you." He swung me into a fireman's carry and started off, bare feet sloshing through the watery meadow.

Oof. I grunted as I landed on his shoulder. He was right: it wasn't comfortable, but it was the best way we had to get me to dry ground since I was still shaking too much to stand up and walk.

CHAPTER FIVE

Becks led the way, taking advantage of high spots while heading toward the game trail that would lead us back to the main hiking trail. The good news was, the closer we got, the drier the ground was.

Sam stopped on a hillock at the edge of the meadow and set me down on the grass before shrugging off his pack.

"Becks, get the towel, sweatshirt, and extra pair of socks from Sin's pack. Get the towel from yours as well. Sin, we need to get you toweled off and into dry clothes." He was rummaging in his pack as he spoke, pulling out a towel, a sweatshirt, and a pair of gym shorts with a drawstring waist. "Thank God the packs are waterproof."

"I-I d-d-d-d-don't k-k-kn-know if I-I c-c-can—"

"We'll do all the work," he cut in. "You don't need to do anything."

I squeaked. There was no other word for it. Ms. "Nothing fazes me when it comes to guys" totally squeaked like a mouse at hearing him say they'd undress and re-dress me. Then I blushed.

Becks and Sam were both kind enough to resist teasing me,

although I could see their lips twitching as they held back their laughter.

"All right, Becks, here we go. I'll hold the towel while you get her wet clothes off. All of them; she's too cold to get warm otherwise." With that, he shook the towel to its full length and gazed into the distance, steadfastly not looking at me while Becks got to work.

It felt odd to be handled like a doll while someone else preserved my modesty, and I didn't want to experience it again any time soon. I was grateful that Becks and Sam did what needed to be done, though, because I was in no shape to do it myself. Faster than I thought possible, Becks had me stripped, dried, and redressed.

"Ok, Sam, she's decent." Becks went to work undoing my braid and towel-drying my long, thick hair. "Ugh. Do you have a comb or brush in your pack, Sin?"

I nodded and gestured weakly at its front pocket.

Sam unzipped it and handed Becks my comb.

"Thanks." She started working it through the tangles while Sam outlined a plan for us to get out of here.

"I can carry you for a little while, Sin, but the longer I do, the greater the risk of injury. Plus, you won't warm up as fast. We need to get you walking. I'm also concerned about the aftereffects of using magic for the first time. You should be checked by a medic as quickly as possible." He paused, thinking. "I think we should contact the Rangers and have them meet us on the main trail in a UTV. If I recall correctly, this is the part of the meadow where I have just enough signal to punch a short call through. Otherwise, it'll have to be a text. I also think we should notify our parents that there's been an incident."

I grimaced but nodded. Becks agreed as well.

Sam grabbed his cell phone and stepped a few paces away, until he got enough bars for a quick call to go through. I closed my eyes, soaking up the sun's warmth while he spoke to someone, presumably a Ranger, before signing off. Then I heard him swear. I opened my eyes and saw his thumbs flying over his phone screen.

Becks finished combing out and re-braiding my hair as Sam came back. He sat down and made sure his feet were dry before pulling on his socks and boots. "Gear up, Becks. It's up to us to get to the main trail and as far down it as we can. The Rangers will meet us on it, and your parents will meet us at the station as soon as possible. They're leaving their meeting in Berlin now but it will take them a while to get back here."

Becks pulled on her socks and hikers before helping me into mine. Then she grabbed a short length of rope from her pack before standing up and swinging her pack into place. Once it was settled, she grabbed my pack and hefted it before directing Sam to lash it on top of hers. It was an ungainly solution, but it sure beat trying to carry it by hand.

Sam donned his pack and settled it before pulling me to my feet. My knees buckled as soon as I was fully upright. He caught me and put me in a fireman's carry once again. "Becks, break trail, please." He was asking her to hold stray branches out of our way so they didn't hit us.

Off we went, setting as steady a pace as possible.

CHAPTER SIX

The trip out took longer than the trip in, because Sam was moving slowly to conserve his energy and not jostle me too badly. When we reached the main trail, I tapped him to get his attention.

"What is it, Sin? Are you going to be sick?"

I was somewhat amused by his question, but it was legit since we couldn't have known how I'd react to being carried upside-down for any length of time. "No, not that. Stop and put me down when we reach a spot with full sun. It'll help me warm up."

I was happy to realize my teeth weren't chattering as badly, although I still had to fight to get certain words and longer sentences out clearly.

"Ok, can do. We should be coming up on a spot soon."

Becks dropped back to walk beside us now that she didn't have to worry about holding branches out of our way. I could feel her assessing gaze on me, although it was several minutes before she spoke.

"There's a clearing roughly a hundred feet ahead of us. Once your head and body settle, I want you to try walking. I'll make sure you don't fall. Don't overdo it, but moving around should help you warm up faster."

By the time she'd finished speaking, I could feel the sun beating down on me. It was a very welcome change from the shade on the game trail.

Sam carefully set me down on a large rock at the side of the trail. I braced my hands against my knees and let my head hang as I adjusted to being upright. Once I was sure the dizziness had passed, I straightened up and told Becks, "Let's try it."

She walked directly in front of me and held out her hands, wrapping them around my wrists as I did the same with hers. "On three. One, two, *three*." I heaved myself to my feet while she tugged me up. It wasn't graceful and I swayed more than once while trying to find my balance, but she held me steady until I could stand without resembling an inflatable wind dancer.

Sam shifted, but Becks waved him off. "I've got this. You rest. You may need to carry her again." Becks retreated to arms' length in front of me, still holding my wrists. "One foot in front of the other, Sin. I won't let you fall."

I stepped toward her, never doubting she'd catch me if I started to go down. Becks was a hell of a lot stronger than she looked.

My legs were shaky and my balance practically non-existent, but I managed to step forward. She retreated to arms' length again. We repeated this process several times until I was steadier. Becks let go, although she stayed close as I slowly paced back and forth in front of the rock. I still had intense zings hitting random nerves in my legs at odd times. Each time it happened it caused me to miss a step and stiffen, almost falling. Becks was quick to catch me every time.

Sam stood up as I neared the rock again. "Time to go. Ready, Sin?"

"As ready as I can be."

"Need a lift? Or are you ready to try walking?"

"Let me try walking. No guarantees, though. I still feel like it's my first day on my new legs."

Becks walked slightly ahead of me on my left and Sam walked behind to my right as we resumed our hike. We weren't covering ground as quickly as we wanted since I was still experiencing random nerve zings in my legs and also needed to stop frequently to rest, but we were making progress.

About thirty minutes later, we heard the distinctive sound of a UTV. It crested the ridge in front of us and stopped.

Two Rangers hopped out and hurried over. "Are you the three who called for help?"

"Yes," Sam answered. "Sin," he gestured at me, "wound up almost fully encased in ice. She's recovering and is now able to walk for short stretches on her own but is still experiencing random nerve zings in her legs. We're also concerned about other possible after effects."

"All right. Get in, and we'll get you back to the Ranger station. We've got one of our medics coming in from one of the other stations. She'll evaluate you, Sin, and decide if hospital treatment is necessary. We'll also need to get a full report about the incident." He gestured toward the UTV.

We walked over and climbed in. Becks and Sam still had the backpacks on, which made sitting very uncomfortable for them, but there wasn't room for them to put the packs at our feet. The Rangers climbed in, fired up the UTV, and off we went.

CHAPTER SEVEN

When we reached the Ranger station some time later, the medic
—another Ranger—was waiting for us. Sam helped me out of the
UTV, steadying me until I found my balance. The medic ushered
me into the station, asking me the standard preliminary questions as we walked. When I told her what had happened, she
stopped in her tracks.

"Ice started spontaneously building around you, then created
a wall between you and a moose?"

"Yes."

"And you've never had anything like that happen before?"

"No."

"Other than the encounter with the moose, was there
anything different than usual today? Something you did, or
maybe something you wore?"

I started to shake my head, then stopped. "Maybe?" I thought
about it for a minute. "I wore my nana's medallion today. I had it
in my hand when the ice started forming."

A thoughtful look crossed her face as she proceeded with the
exam. Once she'd finished, she had me wrap up in a thermal
blanket. The extra warmth was welcome since I still felt chilled.

"The good news is, you seem to be recovering well. I'm going to monitor you until your parents arrive. As long as your recovery continues like this, you should be able to go home rather than to the hospital. If you feel an increased chill, start shivering, or experience a headache, nausea, or anything of that nature, tell me immediately."

"Okay." A wave of exhaustion swept over me.

"You can lie down on the cot to rest."

I shuffled over to the cot, blanket still wrapped around me, and curled up, my eyelids immediately closing as I slipped into a light doze. I could dimly hear Becks and Sam talking to the Rangers, the medic's voice punctuating the conversation.

The medic shook me awake some time later. "Your parents should be here soon. Do you feel up to answering a few questions while we wait?"

I sat up and rubbed my eyes before pulling the blanket back around my shoulders. "I guess. What do you want to know?"

"You said you wore a medallion today and had it in your hand when the ice started forming. Can you tell me the exact circumstances? Everything you remember; it may be the key to figuring out why that happened."

I spoke slowly, sifting through my recollections. "We were lying on the grass near the stream that borders one edge of the hidden meadow, drying off after going wading. I heard the shutter on Becks' camera and her telling us to look to our left. When I did, this huge bull moose was staring at us from about fifty feet away. He lowered his head and antlers and started walking toward us. Sam, Becks, and I all kind of lost our heads and jumped up to scatter, hoping he'd leave us alone—except I couldn't move once I was on my feet. I remember I had the medallion in my hand when the cold hit, and then it was just ice,

ice, and more ice. It got so cold so fast, it wasn't funny. Mr. Moose headed toward me, but just before he reached me, an ice wall came up between us. Don't ask me how; I've got no clue."

The medic's expression never changed but her eyes revealed that she was both alarmed and curious. "May I see the medallion?"

I hesitated before drawing it out from under the sweatshirts, holding it in a closed fist once I had. For some reason, I was reluctant to let her look at it.

My parents rushed through the doorway a moment later, asking me if I was okay. To my surprise, Nana was with them. She immediately pushed her way through the others to sit next to me on the bed, wrapping her arm around my shoulders.

"Put it back under your shirt, Sin." She made eye contact with my parents. "I'll answer any further questions the medic has."

I did as directed without question and was relieved when it was hidden again.

If the Ranger was surprised, she didn't show it. "May I assume you know exactly what the medallion is and does?"

"You may. It's an artifact that's been in my family's direct lineage for centuries. It has two peculiar properties: one is that it chooses who its next bearer will be, and when." She paused.

"And the second?" the medic finally prompted.

"The second is that it unlocks any latent magic the bearer possesses." Nana left it at that, keeping her gaze on the medic.

"An artifact like that should be stored under lock and key where it isn't a temptation or danger to others."

"I assure you, Ranger, it's carefully monitored at all times. Those who need to know about it, know." Nana paused again. "I strongly suggest you refrain from pursuing the matter. Any information beyond what I just told you is need-to-know."

The medic acquiesced with a nod. "Very well, but please make sure the young lady gets the necessary training as quickly as possible. From what she and her friends said, she's lucky she's not seriously injured—or dead."

Nana nodded. "Now that her magic has manifested, her training will begin in earnest." She stood, beckoning me up as well. "Leave the blanket, Sin. The Rangers will need it another time. We have blankets in the SUV if you're still cold."

I folded the blanket and set it on the cot before straightening to face the medic. "Thank you for taking care of me."

"Be well, Sin, and learn quickly. Until later." She walked out, closing the door behind her.

My parents followed her after hugging me tightly, then Nana and me. Becks and Sam were outside.

I looked at them, confused. "Where are your parents? I thought they were coming too?"

Sam answered first. "No, just yours. I texted mine while the medic was checking you over. Once they learned your parents were en route, they decided there was no need to add to the crowd."

Becks followed up quickly with, "Mine said the same but asked me to come home as soon as possible. They're a little spooked." She made eye contact with my nana. "My parents wanted me to ask if we could all come over to talk once you've got Sin home and settled." She glanced at Sam. "Sam, they'd like you there as well."

They both looked at my nana, waiting.

"Why don't both of you come straight to the house? Call or text your parents, Becks, and have them head over. Sam, please let yours know you'll be at our place. We all need to chat while events are still fresh in your minds." She held up a hand when Becks started to speak. "Sin will be fine. She'd insist on being part of the discussion even if she wasn't."

I flushed because she was right.

Sam spoke up. "Becks, why don't you ride with me. We'll bring Sin's backpack since it's still lashed to yours and meet everyone at the house. You can let your parents know before we hit the road."

"Sounds good. Sin, we'll see you at your place." They waved goodbye to everyone, grabbed all three packs, and headed for Sam's car.

Nana turned toward our SUV and gestured to my parents and me to get in. My dad took the driver's seat. Nana and I climbed in back, leaving the front passenger seat for my mom.

"No questions about what happened until we're all at the house." Nana spoke peremptorily as we headed home.

I grabbed one of the blankets on the seat and drew it over me to block the cold air from the AC and leaned my head against the window. I dozed off during the short drive but was jostled awake by the SUV bouncing and swaying over the potholes and ruts at the end of our driveway.

We all got out while Sam pulled in and parked right behind us. Becks grabbed my pack, and she and Sam caught up as I reached the back door. We all went inside. Becks dropped my bag in the mud room on her way in, then greeted her parents when they walked through the door a moment later.

Nana ushered us all into the living room. "Pull up a chair and get comfortable. The kids will tell us what happened."

CHAPTER EIGHT

Once everyone was seated, Nana waited expectantly while Sam, Becks, and I conferred silently.

Becks started recounting the day's events from her point of view. Most of it matched my recollections until she got to the part about the moose and the ice.

"I had my camera in hand when I noticed the moose walk into the meadow a few hundred yards away. He didn't seem interested in us, so I stayed quiet but kept an eye on him. Next thing I knew, his head came up and he started walking toward us. I snapped some pics as he came closer, figuring he'd stop well short of us, but he just kept coming. When he did stop, he was about fifty feet away. That was when I got Sin's and Sam's attention.

"When the moose lowered his head and swung his antlers toward us, I knew it meant trouble. I think I panicked. I know I can't outrun a moose, but my feet took off and the rest of me went with them. Sam took off as well, but Sin just stood there after getting to her feet. It looked like she had something clenched in her hand but I couldn't tell for sure. Then ice started to build on and around Sin. Everything happened so fast! The moose tried to get to Sin, then a freaking *wall* of ice flowed up between them!"

She stopped for a gulp of air. "After the moose left, I tried to get to Sin. I didn't know what I could do, but I had to help somehow. Sam was the one who calmed her down, telling her the moose was gone and getting her to breathe with him. The ice started melting, and once Sin was free and we could walk without slipping around like drunken monkeys on a slip-n-slide, we headed out. I grabbed Sin's and my backpack, and Sam grabbed his and carried Sin. Once we were on dry ground, we got Sin toweled off and into different clothes. Sam spoke to the Rangers and indicated Sin needed medical evaluation. We were told to meet them on the main trail so we started back. Sam carried Sin until she felt she could walk. Soon after that, the Rangers met us and brought us the rest of the way to the station."

Becks gestured to Sam.

"Once Becks alerted Sin and me to look at the moose, I noticed he seemed more intent on Sin than Becks or me. I'm not sure why. Whatever the reason, Becks and I didn't interest him, even when we took off running. I stopped sooner than Becks did because of that, so I got a pretty good look at what happened next.

"Sin had the medallion clenched in her hand. I'd noticed it earlier when it slid out from under her shirt. When the moose started to become a threat, a blue glow leaked between Sin's fingers. I assume it was from the medallion since I've never seen Sin's hand glow before. The ice formed as Becks described. Soon after the ice wall came up, something in the woods caught the moose's attention and he headed off to investigate. That was when I started talking to Sin, trying to get her to calm down. I'm no magic user, but I've talked to people who are. They all say staying calm is key, so I figured that was the best way to help until we could get out of there."

"Thank you, kids." Nana looked at me and waited.

"I was dozing. I heard the camera shutter, then Becks telling Sam and me to turn our heads to the left. When I did, I saw the moose standing there. He didn't seem angry, just curious. Then something changed and he started getting upset. I got up, but couldn't move after that. The ice was already forming and built up rapidly. When Mr. Moose tried to get to me, a wall of ice somehow flowed up between us. I have *no clue* how it happened but I'd really like to know what the hell is going on, because if this is magic, I refuse to have anything to do with it if it means damn near freezing myself to death!"

I was wound up, the fear and stress of the situation making themselves known.

"Easy, Sin." Sam's deep voice grounded me, as did the hand he rested on my shoulder. "We'll figure it out."

I took a deep breath and held it before letting it out. "Nana? What's going on?"

She pinned each of us with an admonitory stare. "This information goes no further than this room. Swear it."

We did, although it raised more questions.

"I gave Sin the medallion for her sixteenth birthday. That was when the medallion made it known who its next bearer would be." She paused. "Sin is the second-youngest bearer in our family's history."

Becks half-raised her hand. "What does that mean?"

Nana shrugged. "Other than knowing the medallion wanted to be passed to Sin, I have no idea. Based on the past, it's likely something is going to happen that will require magic, specifically hers, to deal with."

"Not reassuring, Nana."

"Magic is only a tool, Sin. Once you learn how to use it properly, you'll do just fine." Sam's calm statement helped me stave off a fresh wave of panic.

Becks' father asked the question that was on my mind. "Does the medallion trigger *anyone's* latent abilities? In other words, should we be concerned that Becks might suddenly gain a magical ability as well?"

"To the best of my knowledge, it only works on those it chooses in my direct line. Nothing says otherwise." Nana's reply seemed to reassure him. Beck's mom appeared to be relieved as well.

I wasn't so sure, though, and Sam seemed to share my uncertainty. I resolved to talk to him about it later.

Nana asked, "Kids, do any of you have any more to add to the story? No? Then I think we're all set here."

Becks' parents stood and got ready to leave. They made sure to thank Nana and my parents, wished me well as they said goodbye, and collected Becks on their way to the door.

Nana had pulled Sam aside and was talking quietly. My parents looked as confused as I felt. We talked quietly for a while before they hugged me, told me to get some rest, and left to take care of some household chores. When Nana and Sam finished talking, he came over to me and wrapped me in a hug.

"I'm glad you're okay, Sin. You scared me today."

I rested my head against his chest. "I was terrified, Sam. Thank you for talking me through it. I'm not sure I'd have survived otherwise. Thanks for carrying me out of there as well."

He chuckled. "Just don't make a habit of it, okay? I'm used to your 'large and in charge' attitude and don't want it to change."

"Hey, now!" I swatted him before lifting my head, a look of mock innocence on my face. "How else is a girl gonna get a guy to carry her around?"

We laughed and he squeezed me a little tighter. "I'm onto your tricks now, Sin. Next time I'll make Becks carry you."

"That would be a sight! I can hear the comments from other people now."

Sam shook his head in mock sorrow and let me go. "Devious wench. You'd make sure they knew, wouldn't you?"

"Better believe it, Sam."

He wrapped an arm around my shoulders and pulled me in for a quick one-armed hug. "Get some rest. I'll see you tomorrow at lunch. Your nana invited me."

"Okay. See you then, Sam. Get some rest too."

He left, leaving just Nana and me in the room.

"We have much to talk about in the morning. For tonight, rest and finish recovering because starting tomorrow, you'll be diving headlong into your magical education. The next few months are going to be intense and will consume most of your waking hours."

She hugged me, and as she left, she said, "Welcome to your Oriceran heritage."

FINIS

AUTHOR NOTES

Thanks for reading *White Mountains Manifestation*. I hope you enjoyed it.

When we were asked if there was interest in doing an Oriceran Fans Write anthology, I was quick to join the resounding "yes!" that was the collective answer from the fans. Urban Fantasy is one of my favorite genres to read, and the Oriceran universe sparked my imagination. Funny story about that…

WMM was well along in the writing process when a brainstorming post in the Oriceran Fans Write Facebook group generated several other great ideas. While I was happy to see so many, I'd planned to write one story.

What's that quote about "the best-laid plans of mice and men?"

Months later, when WMM was about two-thirds written, an idea from that brainstorming session suddenly sprang to life in my head and screamed at me until I started writing it. It then proceeded to completely upstage this story, becoming the first of the pair to achieve both 'words complete' and 'submitted' statuses. <<shakes head>> Gotta love characters! Much like cats, they do as they will and we're just along for the ride.

Many thanks to Martha Carr, Michael Anderle, and all the talented authors who brought this universe to brilliant life, helped it grow, and then opened the gates to let others add to the magic.

Reader feedback is always welcome. Feel free to drop me an email or connect with me in the Oriceran Fans or Oriceran Fans Write groups on Facebook. Other published work can be found here.

Magia est aeternum.
Tracey Byrnes

BLACK MAGIC MAFIA

BY TIM BISCHOFF

When black magic and organized crime combine to create designer drugs, it's a recipe for tragedy.

The local sheriff's office is outgunned and outmanned, leaving the community vulnerable.

Is there anyone the sheriff can call for help?

Jed is unique. Born of legend and trained in war, but these days bounties pay the bills.

When people in his community start to suffer, there will be a reckoning!

This story is dedicated to my family.

PROLOGUE

The officer looked around the room, aghast. Several teenagers had perished, and the scene seemed unnatural.

They were in the chairs and lying across the couches, and a couple of them were stretched out on the floor, blissful smiles forever frozen on their faces. No violence was visible to explain what had happened.

One of the first things that came to his mind was a group suicide pact, but he recognized several of the kids. They were all from town, and he knew them well enough that he was able to dismiss that thought. Although many of them could be moody, like most teenagers, none of these kids had ever been in serious trouble or shown any signs that might indicate a tendency toward something as radical as suicide.

Earlier that day, half a dozen parents had come in to report that their kids had not been home in well over twenty-four hours. Alerts had gone out on the teens who were missing, and Dispatch had sent him to this abandoned house after an anonymous tip.

His gut told him that something very unusual had happened here. Even though this was a small rural town in Kentucky, magic sometimes appeared here. Oriceran and its inhabitants had been public knowledge for some time now, but you could never predict how things like that would affect people. As a sheriff's deputy who spent most of his time out in the woods, he saw some strange things. Usually, you just chalked them up to exhaustion or working too many double shifts, but this deputy had long suspected there were things out in the woods that were not easily understood. He was just a guy trying to do his job, and this was way above his pay grade. Folks much higher in the command structure would run this investigation. They were in for a hell of a shock, that was for sure. He was glad he wouldn't have to try to figure this one out.

CHAPTER ONE

I was sitting at the bar nursing my drink when three men walked through the door. They looked as out of place here as a working girl in the front pew at Sunday morning Mass. Nobody comes into a redneck bar like the 5th Wheel in a suit and tie, but it wasn't just their sense of fashion that set off my warning bells. I could sense the stink of darkness on them. It permeated the air around them like a cloud.

Stacey, the bartender and owner, saw the expression on my face and knew something was up. She had also noted the strangers, who had no business being in her place. Of course, she knew a few things about me that most others didn't since she had Oriceran blood in her family. She is a looker with an attitude she can back up. A lot of men have learned the hard way to leave her be unless she requests attention.

I like to keep it on the down-low, being a class five bounty hunter. I am not entirely human either and have been around for more than a few centuries. My mother was a Cherokee who became friendly with a Sasquatch once upon a time, if you know what I mean.

Now that magic is more openly accepted, I don't have to hide my heritage. I got my mother's height out of the deal, which sucks since I'm only about five foot eight. So much for being the son of a bigfoot.

The upside of all this is having a seriously long lifespan, but since I've never met any of my father's people, I don't know much about that. Fast healing I can attest to, from everything I have encountered so far. I can move silently and unseen through the woods when I want to like a Wood Elf, and when I concentrate, I can feel animals' intention and emotion, and sometimes that of the land. So far, no bounty has ever escaped me on my home territory. If something flees into the woods, regardless of species, I can always find it, but the city is a whole different story.

"Jed, I don't like the feeling I am getting from that group that just walked in. They stand out in too many wrong ways," Stacey said.

"They stink of rot and darkness," I replied.

"Keep an eye on them. I'll let the boys know to stay clear of them," she replied with a smile.

I nodded and said, "I will try to keep the damage down to a minimum if the worst happens."

The boss and his two stooges had taken a table in the back of the bar. My intuition screamed that they belonged to one of the dark families, maybe out of Lexington, meaning they were a combination of dark wizards and Cornbread Mafia—something that had taken on a whole new meaning in the years after old Johnny Boone had been taken down as the leader of the original Cornbread Mafia. These dark families were mixing magic, Oriceran plants, and drugs to raise fast money, with no thought to the destruction it would bring into this rural area. They probably figured there was no one around who could stand up to them.

The boss looked like a real douche. He had a slick-looking goatee with the mustache ends curled way up, and he carried a gentleman's walking cane. I was sure he thought he was every-one's better.

Ignoring the hired help but not losing sight of them, I addressed Mr. Big Shot curtly.

"Howdy, fellas. The boss lady was thinking you might be lost and needing directions. Anywhere I can help you boys get to?"

The boss bristled, and his two watchdogs obviously wanted to teach me some manners. Mr. Big Shot quickly got himself under control, however, and said to me lazily, "I am John Fowler," as if he expected that to mean something.

It did, but I wasn't about to let on that I knew him as "Baron."

"My associates and I just happened to stop by this fine estab-lishment for some libations before moving on. I assure you, our time here will be short."

"See to it that it is, and make sure your associates don't do anything stupid. I know what they are and I can handle anything they throw at me," I shot back at him.

It is the unknown that causes most jackoffs to pause, because they're not sure who has the upper hand. Fowler's eyes focused on the door behind me before they darted back to me.

"I believe it is time for us to leave. I require nothing from you." His words dripped contempt. I quickly glanced over my shoulder but missed whoever it was Fowler had seen at the door. "I am sure our paths will cross in the future. What did you say that your name was again?" he asked as they headed out of the bar.

"I didn't. My name is Jedidiah Woods, Baron."

CHAPTER TWO

Sometimes the fastest way to stop trouble is to spot it before it starts.

Stacey looked at me with raised eyebrows as the trio headed out the door. "Not sure what they were up to here, but at least they are gone now," she said.

That damn woman could speak volumes and hardly say a word. "Yeah, but I know we ain't seen the last of them. Not sure why they were here, but something is up."

"Nothing you can do about it now, Jed. Just wait and see what comes around. You know I don't like you starting trouble in here. You can finish it when someone else starts it, but that's all."

I knew there was no arguing with her. She was more than just a rocking body with legs that didn't stop. Her family was a long line of Celtic witches. Unless I wanted some pain-in-the-ass hex on me, it wasn't smart to push Stacey too far in her own place.

The rest of the night went pretty much like most weekends: I drank a lot and busted a few heads when they didn't play by Stacey's rules. I liked this side job; it let me see Stacey when my day job didn't interfere. The regulars were all great, even if the younger ones liked to brawl too much. They were mostly okay, though, as long as they kept it outside and didn't involve weapons. That was just a small-town Saturday night. Hell, we still closed at midnight.

It was early Sunday morning, and my head was aching when I slowly sat up on the cot. I might heal fast from physical damage, but it still took time for booze to exit my system.

Can't say I cared for the view as the night before slowly came back to me. I usually kept to myself and just enjoyed the music, but last night's heavy drinking had taken its toll.

I often crashed at the sheriff's office a couple of blocks from the bar. I have a good working relationship with the officers there and try to lend them a hand whenever they needed help. To keep things legal, they put me on the payroll as a reserve deputy. My cabin was way back in the woods, and I wasn't about to drive home after drinking all night. Stacey even had a few of the local wives on the payroll who took turns picking up their husbands and friends to see that they got home safely. We watch out for each other around here, as people should, but you don't see it much elsewhere anymore.

I had just grabbed a cup of what passed for coffee in the officer's kitchenette when I heard the radio call. There was panic in the deputy's voice.

"Dispatch, come in! We need everyone over here at the abandoned house on Dry Fork Road. Multiple fatalities, no apparent violence. We are going to need the coroner and forensics. Get me some help fast. The crime scene is insane!"

"Well, Woods, it sounds like you might be useful on this one," I heard Sheriff Head say behind me.

I turned around and looked at Richard. We were not drinking buddies, but we could work together most of the time. I think he liked to bust my balls every so often because I had my bounty hunter license. Bounty hunters were given a great deal of leeway in pursuit of our objectives, which he didn't like.

"Something stinks like a dead skunk in the sun for seven days," I replied.

Trying to enforce the law had become much more difficult in a rural county with magic out in the open, so I understood his stress. Usually, if he were giving me too much grief, I would use the shortened version of Richard. Never could fathom why his folks would have named him that, given that last name of his. Of course, it could have been worse. His brother's name was Peter. At least he could stick with Richard. Guess it helped make him as tough as he was for the job he performed.

"I'll meet you over there. Going to cut through the woods and check the outside approach to see if I can pick up anything unusual. Maybe I'll see if my partner is around to lend me a hand," I said with a mischievous smile.

"Dammit, Jed, keep that cat under control around the crime scene! Last time she just about gave old Doc Gant a heart attack sneaking up behind her and squalling like a woman screaming. The damn thing has a wicked sense of humor."

I just shrugged as I headed out the door. There was nothing that I could do to control Elowehi. She did whatever the hell she wanted.

CHAPTER THREE

Elowehi was my companion, my partner, and most of all, my friend. Her name meant "quiet" in Cherokee. We had bonded in a way most people would never understand. Elowehi had a terrible sense of humor and didn't like most humans, so she would do her best to scare and irritate them, just like the sheriff had mentioned.

We didn't communicate with words, but more in mental images, emotions, and intent. I could feel Elo's presence close as I headed across the fields toward the tree line. She was in the shadows, and I got a sense of fulfillment that her morning hunt had been successful. She was unseen, silent death in the woods.

I mentally conveyed feelings of happiness and pride toward her, along with the intent that I would like her to help me with something important. Like I said to the sheriff, she was independent, and unless I was in trouble, I only got her help if she wanted to do so. Most felines had the same attitude no matter what their size. Elo was much more than just an ordinary cat. She was a bobcat and a very large one at that.

While I could tell she was irritated with me as usual, she sent back that she was willing to help. I guess my sense of urgency'd had some effect on her. She appeared out of thin air beside me, and we headed to the abandoned house.

Slowing down about a hundred yards out, I asked Elo to check the area to see if she noticed anything out of place in the surrounding woods. I followed a spiral search pattern inward toward the house.

It was one of those rundown houses that so often becomes a meeting place where kids hang out doing things they shouldn't. The roof and walls were still solid, but the paint was weather-faded and the openings were all boarded over, except where kids had pulled them off to make an opening. I didn't spot anything unusual as I made my way to the back, where Deputy Boone was standing guard over the scene. Doc Gant, the local coroner, was pulling up out front, and I could see the sheriff's Bronco already parked, so he must have entered the scene already.

"Hey, Bill. I heard it was a rough one," I called to the deputy. He just looked at me and nodded. I could see in his eyes that he would have trouble sleeping for a while. It was never easy when it was a kid you found, much less a bunch of them at once. I put my hand on Bill's shoulder and just nodded back to him.

I stepped into the kitchen, noting empty beer cans and liquor bottles scattered all over the place. Nothing unusual for this type of hangout, but when I reached the entrance to the living room, I was stopped in my tracks by the scene.

All the kids had this crazy expression of what I could only describe as ecstasy on their faces. It was an eerie sight to behold. Closely scrutinizing the room, I saw more empty cans and bottles all around, and on the battered coffee table were rolling papers.

Some of the kids were on an old couch and in some chairs, with a few on the floor also. I quickly investigated the other two rooms, but there was nothing in them except a couple of old mattresses. The house was a place to drink, get high, and have sex.

Doc Gant had made her way inside by the time I finished. The place brought forth in her the same reaction that the rest of us had already experienced. She greeted Sheriff Head and turned to me with a much less friendly look. I knew what was coming before her mouth even opened.

"Jedediah Woods, that bobcat of yours had better mind her manners! The last time she took ten years off my life, and I damn near had to change my britches! I will tan your hide and skin hers for a pair of mittens if that happens again!" She emphasized her tirade with a harrumph at the end.

I meekly replied, "Yes'm, I do apologize for that. I don't think she liked your tuna fish sandwich much."

"Don't you sass me, boy! I didn't ask that critter to help herself to my lunch." She said this with a small grin. I knew that she liked Elowehi despite all the bluster.

Doc Gant was pushing sixty, I would guess. I remember when she first came to Marion County and opened her small practice. She had bright red hair and only stood about five feet tall, and she was as thin as a pond reed. That little lady didn't back down from anyone or anything. She had spirit and a caring heart everyone respected.

Sheriff Head spoke up while trying to suppress his laughter. "Doc, have you seen or heard of anything like this before?"

"Now, don't you be rushing me either, young man! You already know I will not guess before I fully examine this whole scene and run all the lab work," she stated clearly. "I suggest we get a rush from the lab on those ziplock bags, although I don't think alcohol had a thing to do with this tragedy."

Sheriff Head meekly said, "Yes, ma'am." He thought that this woman was a force of nature just like we all did.

"Sheriff, you mind if I take a closer look at the baggies?" I asked, and he handed me a pair of gloves as a sign of approval. I carefully lifted the bag to my nose and caught the scent of dark magic. I closed the bag back up, not sure what had changed this weed.

"Tell the State boys to handle this with care and get their magical consultant on it as soon as possible. I smell dark magic on it, but I don't know what it is," I directed. "In the meantime, I am going to head back outside and see if Elowehi has found anything. I'll let you know what turns up."

I carefully slipped a sample I had snitched from the bag into my pocket, figuring I would check it out with my personal consultant. That is, if Stacey would do it. She was about as stubborn as Elo. Well, maybe more so if I'm honest. Females leave us men confused and chasing our tails most of the time, but I enjoyed mysteries even if they often left me befuddled.

CHAPTER FOUR

As I was leaving the house, I noticed a stubby tail jumping out the window of the sheriff's Bronco. *Whatever Elo did is not going to be good*, I thought, wishing that the sheriff had put his windows up. I sent out my displeasure to Elo. I must admit the scolding was combined with amusement as I wondered if she found anything that I had missed.

Suddenly I felt a sharp prick in the back of my calf. The little hussy had stuck her claw in me! I could feel her disdain for my judgment about her behavior but hadn't realized she was that close. Guess I was still a little rattled by the scene. Elo looked up at me for a moment, then walked away. After a few steps she looked back, and I could feel her impatience that I hadn't followed my better, or at least, that was the way *she* looked at it.

I picked up my pace as Elo cut off to the right side of the house and around the front. There sat a jacked-up blue Chevy 4 x 4 Sierra and a small red Toyota Camry—the kids' vehicles, I assumed. Next to the door was a track I recognized immediately, along with a pungent scent. It was light enough that a normal wouldn't catch it, but overpowering to Elo and me. Pukes, I thought in disgust. *"Pukwudgies"* was what the Delaware Native

Americans called them, along with a few other tribes, but I found "Pukes" a very fitting name.

Pukes were a form of goblin two or three feet tall, gray-skinned, with large ugly pointed noses and ears. Those ugly bastards looked like a small person with a bad case of rickets, sharp teeth, and pointed ears had starved to death. They could change into large porcupines, and I had heard it said they could control the soul of any human they killed, but I have never seen evidence to back that up. I considered them an infestation that I wanted to eradicate.

Elo let out a menacing hiss in agreement with the emotion rolling off me. The damn creatures were nothing but servants; delivery boys most likely glamoured to appear human. Hopefully, they would give me a lead to the person running this shit show, though I had a prime suspect in mind and the hunt was on!

CHAPTER FIVE

I sent an image of home to Elo. She would know to meet there. It was time to gear up for the coming fight. Cutting across the woods brought me to my cabin. It had started as one-room, but over the last few hundred years, I had added on to give myself plenty of room and modern comforts. I was off the grid and self-sufficient, the way I liked to live. I didn't rough it by any means. I liked my satellite dish and internet connection. Being able to research and stay in touch were essential tools for bounty hunting. Plus, I didn't want to miss an episode of *Forged in Fire*.

Few people had seen the inside of my place in the last couple of decades, but the ones who had were usually surprised at my comfort level. I grabbed a Guinness from the fridge as I headed for my weapons room.

Long life had brought many changes in weapons over the years. I have seen guns develop from the Kentucky Long Rifle to automatics. I was going with a 9mm Taurus 24/7 G2 pistol. They could take a beating and held seventeen rounds. For blades, I grabbed a tactical tomahawk to offset my Bowie/Kukri hybrid, both made in my home forge. I had found early in life I was a natural at blacksmithing, and it helped pay the bills. Last was a

Wilson short-barrel AR9 full auto and a Stubby 9mm AR15 so all the ammo would be interchangeable. This hunt would lead me into tight areas, and the Stubby would allow me to maneuver easily. Filling a pack with extra ammo, water, and venison jerky rounded out my supplies—no need to overload. The phrase, "Ounces equal pounds and pounds equal pain" that I had picked up from the military ran through my mind. The backup I always carried was a Taurus Judge. I had a personal fondness for the 45 LC, and it could chamber 410 shotgun shells. I snatched some C4 plastic explosive and a crossbow at the last second. Nothing like explosives and silent death to make it a party.

It was getting late in the afternoon; time to head back to town. By now Stacey would be at the bar and could hopefully shed some light on the sample I had taken from the crime scene. I headed for the garage where I kept my 1 1/4-ton 4×4 Jeep M715. She was a classic and in great shape.

An overgrown path that ran for a couple of miles helped keep people out of my area. Once the tires hit the gravel road, I picked up speed, arriving in town about forty-five minutes later. Knowing the front door wasn't open at the 5th Wheel yet, I went to the rear, let myself in, and called loudly to Stacey. I didn't want to surprise her and end up on the wrong side of her temper. I had learned in the past that could be painful.

"Up front, Jed." I heard her call as I wove my way through the stacks of beer and other liquor in the back.

Stacey looked good as I entered the main bar room. She was wearing short shorts, a tight t-shirt, and cowboy boots, making my thoughts scatter for a minute until her laugh snapped me back to the present. That damn woman knew exactly how to maximize her assets.

"Distracted by something, big man?" she purred.

"You know it, darlin'." I grinned. "Only thing is, I need some help—but not that kind of help—at the moment."

"You're no fun this afternoon," she stated with a fake pout.

"Sorry, but it has to do with those kids that they found this morning," I apologized.

Stacey went from playful to serious instantly as she waited for me to continue. I placed the sample from my pocket on the bar. It had the basic look of weed. She was an expert on plants and herbs from Earth and Oriceran. If anyone could help solve this mystery, it was her.

She looked intently at the sample before picking it up and rolling it through her fingers, then she raised it to her nose and inhaled its earthy scent. Striking a match to the sample, a bit of smoke wafted up. After inhaling a little, she began to lose her balance. I caught her before she could fall.

"Is this what it takes to get those arms around me?"

"What just happened?" I inquired, worry in my tone.

"It's ok, Jed. I know what you've got there, and it's not good for anyone" she informed me. "Some jackass has mixed local weed and Oriceran nightshade. Get ahold of Doc Gant immediately. Those kids might not be dead!"

We were in luck; the authorities were still waiting for enough transportation to move the kids. I quickly filled in Doc Gant on what Stacey had told me.

"We're on our way to you as soon as Stacey grabs her kit," I said.

"Swing by my greenhouse on the way, Jed. I need something fresh to reverse the effects," Stacey requested as we jumped in my Jeep. Racing down the street, I hung a right on Stacey's road and swung around to the back, where she kept a small greenhouse to raise the plants she used in her potions.

Stacey emerged moments later from the greenhouse holding a large leaf that looked very close to an aloe spear but was deep purple.

I got us moving toward the crime scene. Stacey settled back into her seat and reached into her bag to pull out a mortar and pestle. She turned the large leaf into purple paste, then added other items to the mixture.

Arriving at the scene, we rushed into the front room and Stacey began rubbing the mixture on each kid's forehead. Once treated, she took out her wand and began to speak.

"*Evigilationem Significasse,*" she intoned loudly.

I could see the kids beginning to breathe normally and the eyes start to flutter on all but one of them. I knew then that it had been too long for young Scottie. He wasn't an outlaw kid, but he could be a little wild. He didn't deserve death for being an idiot. I vowed to myself that I would find the person behind this crime.

Medical personnel were working on the kids as they came awake with loud moans and groans.

"They will have a massive hangover, but they will all be ok except the Wiseman kid," Stacey said, her voice cracking with a mixture of anger and grief.

"Gotta look at the good part. You managed to bring most of 'em back from the brink," Doc Gant lectured Stacey. "We will know what to do going forward."

"I don't know who is behind this crap, but they are using Pukes as delivery boys. I'm heading into the woods from here to hunt the pack down. Doc, can you give Stacey a ride back into town?" I asked.

"No problem, Jed. Go do your job," Doc answered.

Stacey and I headed outside so I could find the trail and start hunting before sundown. Stacey is tough as nails, but at the same time, she has a good heart. Not being able to save them all had hurt, but I knew she would be ok after some time to work through it. I felt sorry for the crowd tonight at the bar if anyone did the wrong thing. All that anger would make someone's night miserable.

"When you finish taking care of business, come find me

tonight, no matter how late." Her tone left no doubt this was an order, not a request.

"You know I will. We can drink, mourn, and celebrate," I replied seriously.

"Be smart and come back in one piece or you will wish you had!" she quipped, walking over to the doc's vehicle with an extra swing in her hips.

CHAPTER SIX

I moved silently through the forest as the shadows got longer with the setting sun. Elo set a brisk pace as we followed their trail. I suspected they would be in one of the many limestone caves scattered across the area, with some up in the trees as lookouts for the den.

About seven miles into the forest, I smelled their stink strongly on the breeze. Time to slow down and be on alert. Nothing could fuck up the day more than a giant pincushion dropping on your head. I figured they would be in porcupine form in the trees and goblin in the cave. Night had not fallen yet, and Puke eyesight was much poorer during the day since they were nocturnal creatures.

Cocking and loading the crossbow, I began scanning the trees in search of the lookouts. Moving slow and letting my natural abilities help me blend into the forest, I covered about a half mile before spotting the first one in the nook of an old oak tree, rolled up into a ball with its beady eyes darting around the area.

The sniveling little cowards never did anything alone; there had to be at least two of them on watch. I kept scanning the trees but was unable to locate the second until I glanced at the rock wall farther up and off to the right. The other was in the shadows on an outcropping above a jagged opening into a limestone wall. There would be more in the cave, so it was time to come up with a plan.

I moved laterally through the undergrowth to draw a bead with the crossbow on the ledge and sent Elo an image of the one in the tree, so she would know her target. I got back disdain from her; she knew her job. *Damn feline*, I thought. *Maybe she should have made the plan.*

Now, I sent to Elo as the bolt flew silently from the crossbow. The only noise from the trees was a slight rustling of leaves as I verified a clean hit through the eye on my target. Looking back at Elo's target, I could see the throat ripped out through my optics. Two down, unknown number in the cave.

I moved up close to the cave entrance, staying out of the line of sight. I didn't want to blow the entrance yet since I wanted a backup in case of a tactical retreat, but I placed enough C4 with a remote detonator to close the opening in case I needed it. I stashed my pack, crossbow, and AR15 in the brush because some of the cave might be a tight space. Bullets wouldn't be safe in there; ricochets could make it a really bad day for me. Even with my healing ability, I wouldn't come back from one in the brain. I loaded the Judge with 410 shotgun shells for close work; they had less chance of a ricochet. The tomahawk and Bowie would be the best tools.

The sun had just dropped behind the tree line on top of the knobs, as the locals called the wooded hills in this area. It was time to enter the cave since now I could go in without the light behind me. My eyesight was exceptional even in the dark, so I didn't require night vision equipment.

Moving into the opening low and slow, I adjusted to the gloom. The opening was rough and narrow, causing me to turn sideways as I inched my way inside. After fifteen feet, the passage opened into a large chamber. Stopping, I scanned the area. I counted four of the little goblin bastards. They were stripping the weed from drying racks and putting it in plastic bags, and there was enough of the crap to cause an epidemic. Only two ways to destroy the magicked dope, fire or explosives, and I was all out of matches. This place was going to go boom.

Elo brushed against my leg. I could feel her anger at the Pukes for having invaded her territory. They were working in pairs, and I sent Elo to the farthest from me. She could move in the shadows unseen.

The air in the cave was acrid, the smell like a combination of rotten eggs and sulfur. The stench burned my eyes and stung my nose.

As quietly as leaves falling from a tree, I reached striking distance. The tomahawk flew from my arm straight to the target. Moving swiftly with the Bowie in my other hand, I headed for the second one. The other goblin's face held a look of confusion as I barreled into it. Hearing the thunk of the 'hawk as it buried itself deep in the first target, I slid my blade through the rib cage into the heart of the second Puke.

Elo's scream of attack reverberated in the cave, and I headed toward the next pair. I could see her launch into the face of one. Her razor-sharp claws sliced through her first target's eyeball, causing the creature excruciating pain. Pushing off the first one with her muscled back legs, Elo propelled herself forward, sinking her teeth into the throat of her second target.

I quickly covered the distance, slamming my knee into the chest of the last one still breathing. Pinning it to the ground while placing my knife across its throat, I held back my instinct to kill it. A trickle of sick yellow looking blood ran down its neck when I applied pressure to the blade.

"Tell me who is your master if you want this to end quickly," I growled, but it stayed silent.

This creature knew it was already dead for what it had done, so it was not about to cooperate. Pulling my 9mm, I put a bullet into its right shoulder with precision. The Puke thrashed in severe pain as I kept it pinned to the floor.

"Tell me your master's name or the other shoulder is next," I shouted.

"The dark man, the dark man," it howled.

"Give me his name and I will stop the pain," I replied.

"Baron. The master's name is Baron," it whimpered.

I readjusted my aim and pulled the trigger, sealing its fate. I had suspected the Baron was behind it after seeing him at the bar, so that confirmed my theory. That cleanup would require planning and information gathering. Now was the time to finish this place off.

I made a circuit around the cavern, placing the rest of my C4 charges in strategic spots, and retrieved my tomahawk. Elo was already outside. I took four pics with my phone, then a couple more after I made my way outside to submit for the bounties. Pukes didn't pay much, but any money is good money. I moved off a safe distance before flipping the switch cover on my detonator and mashed the button in satisfaction.

The ground rumbled under my feet, and rock and dust filled the air. As things began to clear, I could see the cliff had collapsed, sealing the entrance effectively. I was sure the C4 had destroyed everything inside, so it was time to head home.

CHAPTER SEVEN

My first text went to Stacey to let her know I was ok, the second to the sheriff with photos to confirm success.

Reaching the Jeep, I put my gear in it and headed for home. I had not forgotten my earlier orders from Stacey. First thing when I reached home was to clean and put up the equipment. Next was a long hot shower. Then I pointed the Jeep back toward town.

It was pushing one in the morning when I pulled around the back of the 5th Wheel. It had already shut down for the night. After slipping through the back door, I headed for the bar. Stacey was drinking a beer with a shot of Hot Damn whiskey. I rapped on the doorframe between the front and back room to let her know I was there. Her wards had already warned her, but like I said earlier, not a good idea to surprise her.

"What did you find out there, Jed?" she asked.

I could tell she was still feeling down about losing the kid and knew what info she wanted.

"Took out six Pukes and destroyed all of their poison, plus confirmed that Baron is the boss. Will be going after him later," I whispered, placing my arms around her as she melted against me.

Her body finally relaxed some, knowing that I had cleaned up the mess for now and avenged the kid.

She spun around and looked up at me, and I leaned in closer. Our lips came together lightly at first, the passion building slowly. We both wanted to remember life after dealing with death. Breaking the embrace, she headed for her office and living quarters in the back. She grabbed a bottle of Even Williams 1783 as she passed the bar and disappeared into her private quarters.

I didn't have to be knocked upside the head to figure out that I was supposed to follow, and I followed quickly.

My problems would wait for another day.

The End
For Now

AUTHOR NOTES

I want to thank everyone at LMBPN publishing, especially Martha Carr and Michael Anderle for making this story possible. I was fortunate last year to have a story published in Tales from the Kurtherian Universe Fans Write Volume Two.

The first story was much different than this one. My father had become very sick, and I stayed in the hospital with him almost every day for over three weeks. Didn't know if he would come home or not at that time, but the result kept him bedridden with a very severe flare of his Alzheimer's. That story was therapeutic in dealing with the situation in ways I would not have believed at the time it was submitted.

I received many responses from people who had experienced the same thing or were also going through it at that time. These people thanked me for helping them. I couldn't believe it. That the emotion of that little story resonated with so many was very humbling. I want to thank everyone that contacted me; you made it possible to continue with my writing, knowing that I had made a difference. Update: My father passed away on September 15th, 2018. I was fortunate enough to care for him at home on the farm. I know it was a blessing to keep him there for my mother during his final days. It was not easy, but I found the strength from friends, family, and fans of that first story to endure the deterioration of my father's health. Thank you.

Several things are real and a part of history in this story. The Cornbread Mafia did exist with Johnny Boone at the head of it and became public knowledge in 1989. https://en.wikipedia.org/wiki/Cornbread_Mafia. The 5th Wheel bar still operates in Raywick, KY. I grew up in this area and know it well.

All of this would not be possible without Erika, Sarah, and Natale. These three talented organizer/authors have done the heavy lifting to make all this come together. They are amazing, and I have been blessed to meet all three. Thank you!

I write these notes at the 20booksVegas gathering and over the last few days where I have talked, laughed and learned so much from everyone. Sometimes when you deal with others online, you wonder how they will be in person. I am happy to say they are just as awesome in real life. A big shout out to all my fellow JIT members. You are a wonderful family, and the journey continues.

Tim Bischoff

JUST A LITTLE MAGIC

BY KAT N SNOW

Talents are funny things. Some have them very strongly, and others have just a bit. Mostly it depends on what you do with them. Do these girls have enough?

DEDICATION

Dedicated to my dad, who had so many sci fi and fantasy books around the house when I was a kid that it was easy for me to transition from fairy tales to them.

CHAPTER ONE

"It's in the eyes. Always can tell that way." Sara took a sip of her drink.

"Oh, please! You don't really believe that, do you?" Her friend Lydia made a face.

"Yes, I do. Look around the room. The guy at the end of the bar—watch his eyes. He isn't comfortable here. You can tell by the way he stares at the top of the bar, then glances up, and his eyes flit from one person to another and back down."

Lydia watched him for a minute and agreed. "Okay, I'll give you that one. What about the one next to him?"

"The good-looking elf? He's taken. Watch how his eyes continually go to the woman across the room. They are together." She grinned.

Lydia argued, "How do you know he isn't just thinking about hitting on her? Why do you think they are together?"

"He isn't nervous; it's more checking to see that she's okay than planning something."

At that point, the woman he'd been watching walked over to the elf, and they got their stuff together and left.

Lydia looked at Sara with a grimace. "Are you sure you aren't using magic on these people?" Sara laughed, "Don't have to. Already told you—it's in the eyes."

Suddenly she looked down at her drink and asked, "The redhaired woman near the wall. Is she still staring at me?"

Lydia glanced in that direction. "Yeah, do you know her?"

"No, but look at her eyes. Something is very wrong there. Let's go."

They finished their drinks quickly and grabbed their bags. Casually walking toward the door, Sara glanced around the room and saw the redhead wasn't there anymore. Where had she gone?

Lydia closed her eyes for a second as they neared the door. "She's outside. Careful..."

Having a small amount of magic in a world where some had a lot could be both a blessing and a problem. Knowing there were others with much stronger magic made you careful. Not having enough magic to do much made you even *more* careful. Sara could read people somewhat with her magic, but she had enough psychological ability that she rarely used the magic. She thought it was rude to read everyone she came in contact with, and it was also exhausting. Sometimes it was confusing as well because she only caught a glimpse of feelings. Lydia could feel more if she concentrated. She also felt intent if they were thinking of something specific. If she wasn't paying attention, it was just mental noise and she ignored it. Neither of them had enough magic to do much more, but what they had came in handy sometimes.

They decided to try the back door. It was closer to where they'd parked anyway, but as they neared it, Lydia stopped. "Nope, she moved back here. Are you sure you don't know her? Stole her boyfriend or something?"

Sara shook her head. She had no clue what the problem was. A table of people gathered up their things as they passed and Sara grabbed Lydia's arm. "Let's walk out with them."

That worked out well; nobody bothered them as they got to the car. In the car with the locks engaged, they thought it was all fine until the voice came from the back seat. "Start the car and drive to the back of the parking lot. *Now!*"

Sara did so with shaking hands. She wondered what the woman wanted with them.

"Okay, which one of you reads minds?" the redhead snarled. Sara and Lydia looked at each other in confusion. "Neither of us," Sara squeaked out.

"Don't lie to me! I know one of you does!'

Sara stared straight into her eyes and answered, "If either of us could read minds, would we have gotten in the car?"

The redhead sat back in the seat. "Fuck. He *lied* to me.

"Okay, what's going on?" Sara relaxed a bit. This obviously had nothing to do with either her or Lydia.

"Never mind. You can't help me." The redhead started crying quietly.

Lydia turned in her seat. "Probably not, but if you tell us what the problem is, we might have some ideas. And what's your name? I can feel you have magic. Why can't you do anything yourself?"

"Oh, I'm Kate. And yes, I have some magic, but I'm a warrior. I don't have anything mental like you two. You want someone killed, let me know. Joke.

"I don't know how you can help now, but I'm out of ideas. I met this guy a few nights ago. Seemed perfect to me, but boy, was I wrong. I didn't know at first, but he was from one of the dark families. When I found out, I walked away. Later I realized my grandmother's necklace was missing. I went looking for him last night, and he just smirked and said he had no idea what I was talking about. The stone is an artifact, and I've got to get it back. I've never tried to use it, and I have no idea what it can do. And it was my gram's! I need to know where he has it. I thought if I

113

could find someone who read minds, they could check him out and tell me. One of my friends said she knew a guy at that bar who knew someone. He said it was you two." She started crying again.

Sara sighed. "It's just a bar game I play. I can get a feeling about someone, but that's the extent of my magic, and it doesn't always work. Mostly I'm used to watching faces, so I've gotten so I can see things about them by watching their eyes. Wait, do you have anything else that belonged to your grandmother? Lydia might be able to at least get a direction from it."

Kate got excited and started looking in her purse. She pulled out a tiny teddy bear. "Would this work? I gave it to her when I was a little girl, so I took it when she died." She smiled sadly and handed it to Lydia.

Lydia sat back, closed her eyes, and concentrated on the bear. She smiled a little. It held happiness. She tried to attach the feeling to the grandmother. "The only thing I get from this is her feeling for you. She loved you a lot. But I'm sorry, no direction."

"Where does this guy hang out? Maybe we could get something from him if we were near him."

Kate's eyes went wide. "After last night, I shouldn't go near him. I'm not sure what would happen! He might get angry, and things could go badly wrong. I don't want to start a war, just get my necklace back!"

Lydia rolled her eyes. "I didn't mean you should! I meant, if we went to wherever he hangs and he saw you across the room, we would be near him and pick something up from him that way. Like, one of us can stroll up near him and flirt a little to keep his attention and… What?"

Kate had held up a hand to stop her and looked from one girl to the other, then explained. "No offense meant, but neither of you looks like the kind of girls he goes for. You both look like nice little secretaries who just got off from work after a long day.

Your hair looks blah, no makeup, and your clothes are just... No, it won't work. You don't look like rich girls out for a good time."

The girls looked at Kate, giggled since they knew what she was talking about. They had only stopped for a drink at that place. Neither had planned on being out for the night.

Sara laughed. "Not a problem. Come with us to my place and I will show you why."

CHAPTER TWO

Kate sat on a white couch looking around in shock. Sara's condo made hers look like a blue-collar starter home. Mostly white and shades of gray, it had a fireplace and an entertainment system that played softly. Kate still hadn't figured out where the music was coming from or where the speakers were, but it sounded like a band playing softly close by.

Sara called from the bedroom, "The bar is stocked if you want something while you wait. We shouldn't be too long."

Twenty minutes later, out walked two women, one dressed in soft black leather and the other in deep-blue suede. The shoes alone had cost a mint. The messy dark-brown bun Sarah had worn was now long shiny curls. Lydia's blonde ponytail was a well-cut side-swept bob. Their makeup was perfect. Both wore simple jewelry that was quite obviously real.

Sara twirled and grinned. "Think this will work?" They posed. Kate felt stupid about what she had said.

Sara's face sobered. "The way you saw us at the bar? We had just gotten off work. It's very casual dress there, mostly because I want to be comfortable when I work and I own the company. It's a specialty card company, so there are only a few of us, but it pays the bills. You might have heard of it? BEA cards?"

Kate giggled. "I've bought several of them. Everyone loves those! I've always wondered what the initials stood for?"

"Well, not everyone." Sara grinned. "Getting an explosion of tiny stars or flowers at a bridal shower or balloons at a birthday is probably fine. Getting spiders from an ex-boyfriend is probably not!" They all laughed at that one. "The initials stand for 'Blow 'em away,' which was what we talked about doing and hoped for when we started the business."

"Why are you doing this, then? I don't have any close friends who would help me with this, and after what I did at the bar, I thought maybe being working girls, you'd understand what it meant to lose something important. But..." Kate looked at them.

"You don't have to be poor to understand family. If I'd lost something my gram gave me, I'd be going crazy trying to find it —and the item is an artifact. Now let's get a move on. We don't have all night!" With that, Lydia and Sara headed for the door, Kate jumping up to join them.

CHAPTER THREE

"Okay, this was where I met him, so it's a possibility. But it will take a while to get in." Kate looked around. The bar must be jumping since the line outside had about thirty people in it.

Sara looked at Kate. "You go in first. Stand at the end of the bar and look for him. If he is there, stare at him and think about the necklace when you see us walk in. As for getting in…"

Lydia walked up to the bouncer and gave him a hug. It was amusing to watch. Even in heels, she barely came up to his shoulder. "Hi, Jimmy! How's it going?" He grinned and hugged her in return, doing the same to Sara. "Wow, it's been a while. Where have the most beautiful girls I know been?"

Lydia turned to Kate. "This is my cousin Jimmy. Jimmy, my friend Kate."

He looked at her and said, "*Three* gorgeous girls! Kate, you have any problems in here, let me know. Any friend of Lydia's is a friend of mine."

Sara turned to Kate and said, "Go ahead on in. Be there in a minute." Jimmy opened the door for her and some of the people waiting groaned. They could hear the crowd complaining after the other two girls finished talking and hugged Jimmy again and were let in.

Once inside, they looked around. Kate was at the bar, and a man was talking to her. Sara softly told Lydia, "Well, that worked out well, as long as she doesn't give us away. That's our guy with her now. I can tell he thinks he's pulled one over on her. His face looks serious, but his eyes say he thinks the whole thing is funny. If he does this kind of thing a lot, he may not even have realized what it was. Let's do this. I will go right, you go left."

Sara walked up to the bar and leaned toward the bartender, giving her low-cut leather shirt just enough tautness to expose more cleavage. It brought the bartender's eyes to her, and also the eyes of the guy who was with Kate, which was what she had been hoping for. As she stood back up after ordering her drink, she made sure to brush against him. Turning slightly, she looked into his eyes and apologized. After getting her drink, she backed off several feet and waited for Lydia.

When they got far enough from the couple, she whispered to Lydia, "Get anything? I did. It's definitely him, and his eyes went straight to my necklace."

Lydia snorted. "Seriously? With all *that* hanging out? To the necklace?"

Sara lifted her chin. "They are not 'hanging out,' as you so rudely put it. They are carefully exhibited to their best advantage. Worked, didn't it? Even though it wasn't exactly what his eyes were drawn to." She grinned. "Seriously, did you get anything?"

"Not really. All I got was a box with other jewelry. No direction, no intent. Not about the necklace, anyway, but he isn't done with Kate. Nothing specific about why, just that he feels like he has her reeled in for something. Maybe more jewelry, but I don't have a clue." Lydia sighed. "Sorry. And um, I think your 'necklace' did its work. Look who is coming this way."

Sara glanced at the bar where Kate had been. She had disappeared into the crowd, but the guy was walking toward them.

"Hi there, ladies. Haven't seen you around here before. I'm Rob. Can I buy you two a drink?" He was smiling pleasantly but looking at Sara's cleavage.

Sara raised an eyebrow. "Eyes are up here, pal, and no thanks."

He chuckled and apologized. "Sorry. I was looking at the lovely necklace you have on. It's very different." And it was, which was why she'd worn it. Instead of being a diamond or other precious stone, it was a deep purple opal set in white gold. But it wasn't an artifact, it was just a necklace. He obviously hadn't taken Kate's for what it was. Why was he stealing them, then?

Sara looked at him in the eyes. "When I was at the bar, I thought you were already with someone." She still got nothing except amusement.

"Ah, the little stalker girl? Just someone I dated once who won't go away. She is always coming up to me about something or other. Did I leave my sweater at your place, or would I like to have dinner at her place? We didn't click, but she keeps coming back!" He had a rueful look on his face. Sara might even have bought that story if she hadn't already heard the truth from Kate —and if he hadn't kept stealing glances at her necklace.

Out of the corner of her eye, Sara saw Kate go toward the ladies' room, so she waited a minute, then said to Lydia, "Ladies' room. Coming with?" She headed in that direction.

Rob told them, "I'll be right here!" as they walked away.

"Did you get anything from him?" asked Kate as they entered.

"Well, he can't keep his eyes off my necklace, and Lydia got something about a box full of jewelry. Nothing specific, though. I thought you wanted to stay away from him?" Sara sighed.

"He stopped me as I walked in. Oddly, he asked me to meet him on Monday at his place. I've never been there, so I had to ask his address. I wasn't sure what to say, but if he has it, it's probably there. I'm supposed to go there at eight for drinks." Kate had a puzzled look on her face. Sara decided not to mention the sweater she'd supposedly left there. Anger at the lies wouldn't help right now.

"Well, you wait here until I have him turned, so he doesn't see us together. Maybe we can figure this thing out." Sara opened the door.

Rob was talking to yet another woman. Sara watched as he put a hand to the back of her neck as if to draw her closer and then dropped the hand to his pocket. It was fast, and if she hadn't been watching and known what was going on, she wouldn't have understood. She whispered to Lydia, "Aha, that's how he does it!" Lydia had seen it too, saying, "But why?"

As the other woman walked away from Rob, Sara told Lydia, "Make like you are going to the bar. I'm going to talk to this guy. Get close enough behind him to see if you pick up anything." She smiled as she headed toward him.

"Another stalker girl?" she asked him. He grinned. "Who?" Glancing at the woman who had just left, he continued, "No, just a friend. I know most of the people who come here. I'd like to know you better, though. This place is so noisy. I was wondering if you'd be interested in drinks at my place some night? Maybe Monday?"

He gently placed his hand on her neck for a second and Sara knew her necklace was gone immediately, not that she would have if she hadn't seen him do it to the other woman. She gave him a little smile and replied, "What time? And what's the address?"

"Eight-thirty work for you?" He handed her a card with the address. Right after that, she felt compelled to walk away.

CHAPTER FOUR

Back at her apartment, the girls started talking. Sara started. "Okay, I have questions. Kate, after he gave you the address, what did you do?" Kate thought about it. "Um, I just walked away. Yeah, that's odd."

Sara wondered, "Why did we do that? It was like the conversation was done and I had no need to stay. Oh, and I'm his eight-thirty date on Monday. Did you get anything more, Lydia?"

Lydia frowned. "Again, nothing specific. Just vague discomfort, like something was wrong. He was thrilled to get your necklace, but it didn't feel like greed at stealing something expensive. It felt more like he was getting the final piece to something. I think there is much more to this than a stolen necklace."

Sara looked serious. "You're right. I have a friend with the Silver Griffins, and I think it's time I called her. This is more than we can handle on our own. Sorry, Kate, but I think the best thing that ever happened was your friend telling you we could read minds. You aren't the only one this has happened to, as we saw tonight. How many others are involved, I wonder? And what is he doing with all the necklaces?"

She picked up her phone and dialed. "Hi, Mary. I have a story to tell you, and you can let me know what you think."

"Okay," Sara told the other girls as she hung up, "they already know about him, because the idiot did this to one of their daughters. They've been looking into it, but like us, they thought it was only her. Mary will call back as soon as she's discussed it with some other people. Right now, all we can do is wait. Like Lydia and me, this girl only has a small amount of magic. From what you said, you are stronger, right?" She looked at Kate.

Kate shook her head. "No, I said I was a warrior because I know a lot of martial arts. I learned them growing up because I don't have much magic. I look weak, but even a powerful witch can't do much if you kick them in the chin and knock them out. They never expect it. Funny though—I thought I walked away from him because of his family ties, but all of us walked away, and you barely spent any time with him."

The phone rang, and Sara answered. "Wow, that was fast." She was right, it was Mary, who handed the phone to someone else who said gruffly, "Tell me everything you know about this from the beginning!" Sara repeated everything she'd told Mary, then answered several questions with "Yes," "Uh huh," and "I think so." "I agree." she finished. "See you then."

She hung up and turned to the other girls. "They can't let this go. They can't do anything yet, because it's only petty theft as it stands, and they had no way to prove he did it. However, the Monday night dates are what have them worried. Why all of us there the same night? Why did we agree to it in the first place? Normally I never would go after just meeting him. Also, he lied and said you had been there, Kate." Kate started to protest, and Sara said, "We knew it was a lie, but he thought he was making himself look good. Anyway, they are coming over to talk about this and bringing the daughter over, so we will recognize each other if we see her. She's his seven-thirty. They will have someone watching his place from now until Monday, because who knows how many other 'dates' he has planned? But why Monday? They are looking for a reason, but I don't think the day has anything to do with it. I think he was done when he got my necklace. It was the last one he needed."

CHAPTER FIVE

Not long after that, the doorbell rang and Sara let Mary and two other women in. The youngest looked at the girls and said, "All of you? He took something from all of you? How many others has he done this to? And why you? You are all old; you have to be like thirty or something."

The young girl had on way too much makeup and was dressed in a low-cut purple minidress. She still looked about sixteen to Sara, but that didn't mean anything. Hard to tell sometimes how old someone was.

Sara rolled her eyes and shook her head. "And you don't look like you are old enough to have been in a bar!"

The girl looked away. Lydia spoke up, "Remind me to tell Jimmy to stop checking tatas and start checking IDs closer!" Everyone but the girl laughed.

Mary introduced them. "This is Cassidy, and you are right. She shouldn't have been there. She was using Grace's ID that she'd 'borrowed' without Grace's consent, Because of that she almost didn't tell anyone about what happened until her sister noticed the necklace was missing. Grace had given it to her and

Cassidy wore it all the time. This is her sister Grace. They came to me because they didn't want to bring their parents into it. I did tell the parents, but they are leaving it in my hands for now. Like you girls, Cassidy has only a little magic. We are wondering if that's the key to all this. We've checked the guy out, and as far as we can tell, he's never been involved in anything except stupid stuff. Pranks, mostly, because guess what? *He* doesn't have much magic either."

"None of this makes sense, does it?" Sara wondered. "Have the people watching his place seen anything yet?"

Mary shook her head. "No, but we have all day Sunday yet. We'll let you know if we get anything before Cassidy's 'date.'"

"You are letting that kid go?" Sara's eyebrows rose.

"I'm not a kid!" Cassidy started.

Mary frowned at her. "Not really. Grace looks enough like her that in makeup, we figure she can pass. We don't think he actually pays much attention to the girls he picks in the first place, given what you said. It's their magic level and the necklaces."

At this point, Kate joined in. "I've got to get mine back. It's very important to me."

Mary looked at her for a minute. "You're Kate Blake! Did he take your gram's necklace?"

Kate sighed. "Yes. At first, I thought he took it because it has a small artifact as the pendant, but it doesn't look like that now."

Mary giggled. "You haven't ever used it, have you? That's hilarious! I helped your gram with that. It's really just kind of a memory stone. When you get it back, say 'Gram, I have a problem.' Can't believe you never said that while wearing it. She said you started almost every phone call with those words! She figured one day you would say that without thinking because she often did that after her grandmother died."

Kate just looked at her with wide eyes.

"Okay," Mary said, turning to the door. "We will let you know if we hear anything before Monday, but right now there's not much we can do. I'd like for us to all be together on Monday before this starts unless they see other girls going in before Cassidy's slot. We have no clue how many he has coming. Also, that address he gave all of you? He doesn't live there. As far as we can tell, he still lives at home with his parents."

CHAPTER SIX

Sunday was an anxious day. They didn't hear anything from Mary. Hopefully, that meant he hadn't invited a long string of girls for whatever he had planned.

Monday at seven in the evening, Mary called. "Okay, So far it's been quiet there. We've had someone watching all day, and nobody has been in or out. Wait—a girl just headed for the house. We will watch for a few minutes and head in if she doesn't come out. If he has one every fifteen minutes, it shouldn't be long. And…she wasn't in there for any time at all. She came right back out. I will call back. We're going to catch up with her down the street and talk to her."

Twenty minutes later the phone rang again. "This is what we have. The girl walked in, and he told her that her necklace was in a box on the table. She went over, opened the box, saw a jumble of necklaces, and grabbed hers. Then he told her to leave, so she did. She didn't think anything weird happened, but from what we can tell, she has absolutely no magic left. It has to be the box. Since we know this part, we had Cassidy call him and say she'd be late. We can remove her and Grace from the situation. He got very upset but said if she had to be, fine. He might call one of you to come earlier. Probably Kate, since she is his eight o'clock. All of you come down here now. We are in the silver van on the north corner."

Sara giggled. "Silver?"

Mary sighed. "We have lots of vehicles. This one just happens to be silver."

Kate's phone rang. She answered and put it on speaker. Rob's voice pleasantly asked, "Hi, I was wondering if you could make it a little earlier? Something has come up. By the way, I found your necklace. It's here! Must have gotten caught on my jacket that night."

The girls rolled their eyes at that. "Oh, that's great!" Kate answered. "I'll be over soon if that's okay."

Rob was quick with his answer. "Great! Hurry on over!" His charm seemed quite a bit lacking suddenly. Kate hung up and asked the other girls, "Maybe he is in a hurry because he might have to go find another necklace?"

Mary was still on the other phone with Sara. "That will work out perfectly. Make sure you stop at the van first. We are going to go in right after Kate. We need proof. He won't have to worry about another necklace after that."

CHAPTER SEVEN

"Do not touch that box." Mary started as they assembled behind the van. "I don't care what you do; pretend you don't see the opening, or just keep him talking. Walk over to it, look at it, but don't touch it! We figure it's the fact that the girl willingly opened it without being forced."

Kate hurried down the street to the house. Rob let her in with a smile and said, "It's in that box on the table. Sorry about that. I really didn't know I had it."

She looked at the box. It was a pretty little thing with an obvious lid. Saying she couldn't figure out how to open it wasn't going to work. She looked at Rob with a little smile. "Well, I thought we were going to have drinks? I can get it before I leave."

Rob got an aggravated look on his face. "No, I told you something came up. Just take the necklace now."

She felt a real urge to walk to the box and get it and had to fight the feeling. If she hadn't already known he could do that to someone, she probably would have just given in to the urge. Talking to him wasn't going to work either. He looked anxious and a little angry. Suddenly a thought came to her and she said, "Gran, I have a problem."

Rob looked at her like she was crazy, and then a voice started talking. "Girl, you know you can handle anything. What's wrong today?" Kate smiled a little. She had wondered if she actually had to have it on her or just nearby.

Rob looked panicked. "Who is that? Where are they? Who did you bring with you? I didn't see anyone else!"

The group of Silver Griffins came in the door as he spoke and Rob ran toward the back. They had people out at the back, but he didn't go out that way. They checked all over the house, but he was gone. He must have used a portal. However, he had left the box. Mary picked it up wearing a pair of gloves and made sure it didn't open. "We will get your jewelry back to you after we have someone look at this. It isn't listed as a known artifact, so we aren't sure exactly what it does or how it does it. We still have to find Rob and ask him where he got it. Wonder why he ran like that? He had no idea who was coming in."

Kate laughed. "I think he was running from Gram, not you. I didn't know what else to do because he was getting aggravated about me not touching the box, and the opening was obvious so saying I couldn't figure it out wasn't going to work, so I said—"

Mary raised her eyebrows, "You talked to your grandmother?"

"I couldn't think of anything else to do. He was getting mad because I wouldn't get my necklace! The look on his face after she answered me! He was looking all around the room, trying to figure out how someone else had gotten in here. It would have been hilarious if the whole thing hadn't been so scary, but I may have cost us grabbing him. I'm sorry."

Mary shook her head. "He must have had the portal ready in case this whole thing didn't work out. No way he had the ability to just make a portal that fast by himself. As I said earlier, he doesn't have much magic. What he *does* have, probably, is the persuasion ability he used and not much else. We will get him. We already have someone watching his parents' house. The important thing is that we have this box and can figure out exactly what it does. Plus, we'll keep it out of the hands of another jerk like him. Wonder where he got it and how they knew what it could do? Has someone else used this recently?"

CHAPTER EIGHT

Several days went by. Sara, Lydia, and Kate had become friends and called each other about once a day to see if any of them had heard anything or just to talk about their day. It was the weekend again, and they made plans to meet at the same bar they had met at originally.

Kate pulled into the parking lot and turned off her car. She smiled when she saw Sara's car already there. The other two girls must already be inside. She was gathering her things when the passenger-side door opened. Rob jumped in and slammed the door.

"You have to give me back the box," he snarled. "I don't care how you get it, but you *will* get it back. Your little friends won't be in good shape if you don't!"

Fear filled Kate. He mustn't have noticed the Silver Griffins coming in; her gram must have scared him badly. He thought *she* had the box. Just because the girls' car was here didn't mean he hadn't already done something to them. Then she remembered what Mary had said he didn't have much magic either. Could he have enough to overpower both of the other girls?

She decided to try something. Staring at a car that wasn't

theirs, she said, "Their car is here. They are inside, and you haven't done anything."

Rob looked at the car she was looking at and laughed. "I got them getting out of the car. They did what I said. Most people do, you know."

He had no clue which car Sara's was. He was lying. That made things so much easier. Kate made herself sound panicky. "Don't hurt them! It's in my trunk!" She had to get him out of the car so she had room to move.

"Give me the keys!" Rob sounded like he was elated as he grabbed the keys from her hand and jumped out. He ran around to the back of her car and was trying a key. The key that started the car wasn't the same one that opened the trunk, so he fumbled a bit. Kate followed him and while he was intent on the trunk, let loose with a series of punches and kicks that had him on the ground.

Inside Lydia turned to Sara. "Something's wrong. Kate is scared, and she isn't far. It has to be Rob! The parking lot?"

They jumped up and headed for the door. They got outside in time to see Rob laying on the ground with his hands covering his head for protection, while Kate was on her phone calling Mary. "Got him! Send someone to pick him up before I beat the hell out of him! Yes, Rob. He thought I had his precious box. Yeah, I think Gram scared him so bad he ran and never noticed you guys, or he just thought it was another of his women." Kate giggled at the thought. Rob groaned on the ground, and she heard him say, "Your grandmother? What?"

Sara looked at Kate and raised her eyebrows. "I see what you meant about them never expecting it from you! Is he going to live?" She snorted. He was obviously in pain, but other than around his sort-of-crooked nose, there wasn't any blood.

"He will live." Kate looked at him in disgust. "The karate I used is to disable so I have time to run, not hurt someone, although I'm pretty sure he is feeling it! I could have used other moves that would have done more damage, but I know they want to question him. Hard to do that if he's in the hospital or dead."

Rob groaned again and looked like he was thinking about trying to get up. He decided to stay down when a van pulled in. Sara saw who the driver was. "Looks like his ride is here." Mary and four other Silver Griffins jumped out, and Mary looked down at him and raised an eyebrow. "Nice job, Kate. He can still talk! We'll take it from here." One of the witches looked at him in disgust and did something with her wand, and Rob got up and walked to the van. Mary very quietly told the girls, "That's his aunt and she hates his whole family, so this really made her mad. She has more persuasion in her little finger than he could ever wish for. Thanks for calling. We will get back to you when we know something. I'm pretty sure his aunt will have all we need by the time we get home!"

CHAPTER NINE

The girls decided to head back to Sara's place. They really didn't feel like they'd enjoy themselves waiting for the information at the bar. They had just settled in when the phone rang. When Sara answered, Mary began talking. "Okay, the box stores any magic willingly offered to it. We figured it was something like that. All we had to do was turn it upside down and dump out the necklaces. You can come and get them tomorrow. However, there were seven other necklaces in the box, and we may never know who they belonged to. The good thing is, probably the only magic stolen was the first girl's. He thought it would give him the magic it collected, but we doubt that would have happened. However, we also have no information on who made it or how to give that girl's magic back. He bought it from a guy in a bar. No name. Other guy said he'd used it and it worked. I'm thinking the other guy probably had no clue how it worked either and just was getting rid of what he thought was a piece of junk. That was all Rob's aunt could get from him. She's pretty good at what she does, so there probably isn't anymore.

"Anyway, as I said, come get your necklaces tomorrow. At least it's out of Rob's hands, and whoever else might have ended up with it. We are going to work on investigating the box. I'll let you know if we find out anything we can tell you. Have a good night." Mary hung up.

"Well, I'm ready to go back out for a drink after that!" Sara grinned, "Everyone, leave your jewelry here!"

AUTHOR NOTES

Author Notes are hard! Most stories, the characters help you figure out what to write. For *Notes*, you have to use your own thoughts!

When I wrote this, I was thinking about how most people in this universe were powerful in one way or another. What if someone only had a little magic? How would they use it?

Thanks to Michael Anderle and the other authors for allowing us to use their universe.

— Kat

A CONFLUENCE OF METAL AND MAGIC

BY TR CAMERON

Dark magic arises in yet another city, and a new team of agents assembles to fight it.

Combat experience: significant. Magic experience: less significant.

Who better to lead them than no-nonsense, highly experienced Agent Diana Sheen?

It's a new gig in a new town with a mostly new crew.

Sheen can count on her right-hand woman Cara Binot and not much else when it turns out there's a jailbreak planned.

The culprit? A seven-foot-tall, dark-magic-using demonic-seeming menace who calls himself "The Fallen." It will take magic, guns, and a lot of luck to bring him down, especially with an unproven team backing her.

Because reports suggest he likes fire—a lot.

And the jail? It holds prisoners with deep wells of dark power and the ability to use them.

Taking him out is a mission she can't refuse.

It's going to be a blazing hot time as Sheen heads into the monster's lair!

DEDICATION

For Dylan.

A CONFLUENCE OF METAL AND MAGIC

"I hate those pretentious bastards," Diana Sheen groused as she entered her office and threw her briefcase at the bench by the wall. It missed, and she stared at the traitorous item while it fell, then turned to regard the other person in the room.

The compact blonde on the visitor's side of the stylish glass desk laughed. "You mean the oversight committee actually wants to exert oversight on us?"

Sheen slipped into the expensive leather chair across from Agent Cara Binot and leaned back, closing her eyes. "Exactly. 'Miss Sheen,' they say—it's always Miss, of course—Miss Sheen, can you explain why your division's new location needs so much budgetary support?'" Her impersonation of the committee's head elicited another bout of laughter before she continued in her own voice. "Why yes, Mrs. Chairperson, it's because a new fucking realm made itself known in the not-too-fucking-distant-past, and each year more rogue elements cross over to threaten our way of life. Perhaps you could quit asking me stupid-ass questions and let me go do my job before you find the blessed Golden Triangle overrun with creatures out of legend and a damn dragon or some other bloody monster taking up residence at the gods-damned confluence, hmm?"

"I hope you were more politically correct than that, Boss."

"I may have used slightly less colorful language."

"So, are they freezing us?"

"That's the best part. They know if they tried, they'd be totally screwed. We need an office in Pittsburgh, given the off-the-charts magical power base or whatever the hell it's called here, so of course, they approved the request. They just needed to make sure to put me in my place. A farce. An absolute bloody farce."

"If only they knew the truth."

"Ha. Assuming they were capable of recognizing truth if it bit them, it would be a disaster. They can't cope with reality, which is why they try so hard to avoid it. So, I'll keep jumping through hoops until the time comes to tell them that they can kiss my shiny metal ass."

She blew out a breath and sat forward in her chair, rotating to face Binot. "So, what's *your* complaint today?"

"We need more people, including a WMW." The government loved acronyms, and a think tank had designated those strong in magic as Witch/Mage/Wizard to avoid offending anyone. Naturally, they had succeeded in offending everyone.

"Half the team has strong magic."

"Let me put it this way: right now we have the magical capacity to take down mid-range enemies, but—"

"But we're not facing mid-range. I get you." Sheen sighed. "It's ironic that we've got the funds to hire but can't find the talent. What a mess." She drummed her fingers on the table. "Suggestions?"

Binot shrugged. "If Kettner works out, we could consider more investigators from the Army's police."

"And how *is* Kettner working out?"

Binot checked the time and grinned. "Actually, Ninja and Glam are about to run him through the course. Wanna watch?"

"Anything to get out of this damn office before another Washington reptile calls me. Let's go. Fast."

"Three sentries in position ahead," said the far-too-young-sounding voice of the team's electronic ghost, Kaleigh Dornan.

Trent Parker acknowledged with a pinky tap of the comm stud on his glove and glanced up to see the tiny drone hovering above, almost invisible in the darkened heights of the warehouse.

Their targets were in the back corner. The rest of the cavernous space was a maze of stacked cargo containers. It was a ludicrous tactical situation, but "ludicrous" had become the new normal.

The glasses he wore linked wirelessly to the combat computer on his belt and provided an augmented reality view of the enemy guards. He whispered, "Khan, you have number one. Kettner, run past and take the second. I'm on three. Don't miss." The leapfrog tactic was less than ideal, but time was a factor. "Go on my mark." He paused to see if the universe would provide him with any additional suggestions. It didn't. "Mark."

Khan broke out of his hiding spot in the shadow of a container stack and ran for the ninety-degree angle in front of them. Kettner was two steps behind. Parker moved forward in a shuffling crouch, rifle seeking opponents above. The drone would probably identify any such threats, but redundancy was a good thing. His teammates careened around the corner. In their camera feeds, positioned in the extreme right of his glasses, he saw Khan's triple burst drop the first opponent in a clatter of body armor.

The second guard had overwatch on the first and fired at the same time as Kettner. The two traded shots, a controlled salvo from the Army MP and a sustained one from his foe. Kettner's knocked the guard back, but the return volley climbed his body in a diagonal from his thigh to his chest. The big man spun to the ground, his rifle swinging free on the end of its sling.

Parker swerved to avoid his fallen ally and engaged his attacker. He was running too fast to aim, so instead, he swung the rifle's stock around, smashing him in the solar plexus as he passed. The guard collapsed to his knees, temporarily out of the fight, and Parker trusted that Khan would finish him. He rounded the corner to find the third foe waiting and slid to dodge the fire that was sure to be coming. His silenced weapon spat out a triple burst, hitting the enemy in the thigh, torso, and throat. The man staggered and slumped against the nearest container.

Parker rolled up to his feet, smiled at the subdued man, and raced on. Unfortunately, the drone had not spotted the tripwire, and neither did he. When he crossed it, deafening explosions filled the maze. His body locked up and he dropped to the ground.

Binot walked into his line of vision and knelt to gloat. "Got you."

He sighed. "I guess it's true, what they say. There *is* a first time for everything."

"Unfortunately, Sheen got called away on our way down. Otherwise, she would have gotten to enjoy the sight as much as I did." Binot hit a control on the tablet she held, and his training suit released and allowed him to move again. Trying to do so without the electronic all-clear was something a person only did once. The electroshock punishment was ferocious. He took the offered hand and pulled himself up with an audible groan. She laughed and he glared with mock fury, then dropped the act.

"What was it?" He secured his rifle, which shot laser light instead of projectiles, setting it across his chest in the ready position.

"Hyper-directional ultrasonic sensor. Anyone moving faster

than a slow walk would have set it off." Binot motioned for him to follow.

"Seems impractical." He stayed a step behind her as she walked back through the maze, releasing those still trapped by their training gear.

"Reports are that the Oricerans deployed something similar in a recent fight, although they used spikes rather than a light show, and almost certainly magic sensors instead of tech."

"Ouch." He shuddered theatrically.

"Right? Plus, of course, the spikes were thrown by some kind of magic. Give me good old reliable and predictable gunpowder any day."

Dornan's voice interrupted their chatter. "We have a problem. Boss wants you in the situation room."

Ten minutes later they were in what passed for an everyday uniform at the Agency, a mix of denim, sports, and tactical wear, and other personal odds and ends. Anik Khan wore the photographer's vest that was the non-combat equivalent of the tactical demolitions gear used in the field.

"It took you long enough," Sheen observed with a frown as the foursome entered the situation room in a line.

"Everybody died. Had to revive them." The humor in Binot's voice was unmistakable and drew a laugh from Sheen.

"Speaking of dying," Dornan interrupted, breaking the mood, "take a look at this." From her position in the corner surrounded by a curve of computer monitors, she triggered the displays that covered the walls of the room. They showed an image of a skyscraper fed by one of her many drones as it circled the building. "An informant tells us the top floor houses a person of interest—a level-five bounty that calls itself "the Fallen." She made a dismissive noise. "Stupid name."

"Brownstone's not available?' Kettner quipped.

"He doesn't make it to Pittsburgh all that often, it seems," Binot replied. "That's one of the reasons we're here."

Sheen nodded.

"Guess we'll have to take care of this *pendejo* ourselves." Parker's voice transmitted his eagerness to engage. "What do we know?"

Dornan replaced the uniform feed with different data routed to each monitor. On one, their target glared at them from an official-looking photo. In others, facial recognition had caught him at various activities in the city, none of them notable. Binot approached a monitor that triggered her instincts. It was a file page bearing the logo of the Oriceran consulate.

"Holy hell. Says here that he's telekinetic and pyro-transgenetic."

"What now?" asked Khan.

"He can bind fire into shapes," Dornan explained.

Sheen crossed her arms. "That's pretty fucking impressive, all right. Let me just say that I love this town and the opportunities it presents for us to preserve the common weal." She turned to face Dornan. "So why is he suddenly too important to wait until we're fully operational?"

"The Oricerans gathered intel suggesting he's planning to liberate some friends from the Cube." The prison for the magically active beneath the north shore of the city was a closely-held secret, so his knowledge of it was troubling. That he planned to engineer an escape was a catastrophe in the making.

"Do we have enough evidence to move?" Franklin Kettner, the investigator seconded from Army Military Police to help launch the new office, was the unit's legal conscience.

"It's all on the up and up," Kayleigh replied. "Warrants and everything."

"That was fast." He smoothed his mustache with a knuckle, left side first as always. Sheen smothered a grin at the habit.

"It pays to have friends," she said. "Okay, any concerns before we go?"

There were none.

"Then get your lazy asses to the bus, people. Move."

The rolling command post was about three-quarters as large as a standard semi-trailer and had several skins that could deploy at the touch of a button. Currently, it was pretending to be an auto parts delivery vehicle. It had inconspicuous bulletproof armor all around, and the front third could expand to provide more room.

The back two-thirds was a mobile armory. Lockers occupied one wall, and a folding bench latched down on the opposite side. As the driver wove through city streets and earned constant curses and rude gestures, the team geared up in silence, each finding their center for the upcoming battle. The standard Agency combat uniform inspired thoughts of mayhem. Tight black pants featured Kevlar plates covering critical areas, and a thick long-sleeve t-shirt covered them neck to wrists. A wide web belt held a medic pouch, magazine loops, grenades, and attachment points for other essential items. They wore jump boots with metal bracing to improve protection and minimize potential damage.

Atop this base rode thigh holsters, a pistol on the dominant side and baton with electrical discharge capability on the other. A bulletproof vest protected chest and back and offered more attachment points. Straps held light impact shields to upper and lower arms, and a black combat helmet and AR goggles finished the kit. The Agency had experimented with full-head protection that locked into the vest, but operatives had found it too disorienting for close-quarters battle, which this was sure to be.

There was a shotgun or rifle with a chest strap for each team member on the wall by the back exit. They loaded the rifles with alternating armor-piercing and hollow point rounds, and additional magazines of each were in the standard loadout.

Once outfitted, they sat on the bench and watched the feed from Dornan, who remained at HQ. They had discovered early on that some forms of magic could compromise computer gear, so she took part by remote. A network of relays that the advance team had quietly installed on roofs all around the city prior to their arrival offset the lag.

Her voice was soft and carefully calm as she handled the briefing. "The tower is sixty-four stories. The top floor used to be a restaurant, but now it's the home office of Evil Oriceran WMW, Incorporated." An image of the skyscraper grew larger and rotated. "The drones identified the windows on fifty-nine through sixty-four as not-glass. They're metal of some kind, and the analysis software is going haywire trying to figure it out."

"How does that happen?" asked Kettner.

"Wizard did it," answered Khan immediately. "Only, you know, *literally*."

"So rappelling from the roof is out is what you're saying." Parker sounded disappointed.

"Exactly," Dornan confirmed. "We're not blasting through that stuff with anything shy of a missile, and the oversight committee frowns on us borrowing Predator drones to use in domestic territory."

Binot snorted. "Should be called the 'short-sight committee.'" A low laugh came from the front, where Sheen was setting up the team's comms and goggle feeds. "Besides, there are probably traps or surveillance up there. That's what I'd do."

"Is there *any* good news?" Parker asked.

"Well, there's this." Dornan switched to the feed from a different drone. It showed a construction crane working nearby.

"You're not seriously suggesting we use that to enter the building?" Khan did not sound as if he was in favor of the plan.

"Unless you want to walk up sixty-plus flights."

"I vote against that option," said Kettner.

"It's not viable for all of us anyway," Binot observed, "but one or two people could go in that way."

"Anything else?" Sheen asked.

"Nope," Dornan replied. "Heat signatures are about what you'd expect for an office building in the evening, but there's no telling whether they're workers, guards, human, or Oriceran. Once you're inside and deploy the hounds, I'll be able to identify more effectively."

"Okay," Sheen said, "here's what we'll do."

The truck stopped a block away, and the team emerged at a jog. Parker and Binot—Ninja and Croft—moved in the direction of the crane, each carrying one side of a long duffel. The rest headed for the plaza that surrounded the building and knelt in the cover of large potted trees inside giant concrete planters.

"Ground team ready," Sheen reported.

Binot answered. "You know, Boss, you're supposed to stay in the truck."

"Aren't you the whiner who's always telling me we need more people on the team?"

"Not exactly what I meant."

"Quit complaining and do it."

"Right. Standby," Binot replied. She looked up to see that Parker had freed the grapnel. It was a test model, complete with directional fins on the business end that Kayleigh Dornan—Saber —could control. Parker's voice came over the comm.

"All yours, Saber."

"Roger, Ninja. Stand clear." She waited a beat before remotely firing the device. The concussion echoed from the nearby buildings as the grapnel flew up toward the forward portion of the extended arm of the crane.

"Secured," Dornan confirmed.

Binot jogged over and stood next to Parker. He'd already latched the climbing engine to the toothed cable, and he attached double safety lines to her harness before she had stopped moving. He gave her a look to check in and received a nod.

"Croft and Ninja heading up," he announced over the comm, and then they were levitating, or as close to it as she could get. That wasn't her particular talent. It was a unique view, the ground receding as they went up ten stories, then twenty, stopping at forty-two, the point that Dornan's computers had calculated offered the best odds for success.

They clambered onto the arm and separated to their tasks. She pulled a pair of lines, untoothed, out of the duffel and attached them to her harness. Parker pushed down the bipod legs of his sniper rifle and lay prone, his eye to the scope.

"Ready, Ninja?" she asked.

"Give the word."

"Ready on the ground?"

"We're falling asleep waiting for you, Croft," Sheen replied.

Binot sighed into the mic. "Fire in the hole."

The sniper rifle was loaded with armor-piercing rounds powerful enough to smash the safety glass of the "ordinary" floors of the building. They had chosen a floor several levels down that was devoid of heat signatures as their target. Parker fired a trio of shots, shattering the obstruction and opening a wide hole.

"Are you sure of this cable length, Saber?" Binot asked, tugging on the carabiners that held it secure around the end of the crane arm.

"Math never lies," she replied immediately.

"You didn't forget to carry a one or anything?"

"Are you seriously questioning my math skills?"

Parker had swapped his sniper rifle for the standard kind and fired a grenade on a long arc into the building. It billowed smoke and triggered the fire alarms. "Go, Croft."

With a grin and a wave, she dashed away from the skyscraper and jumped into space.

———

At Parker's "Go, Croft," the ground team erupted into action. They flowed toward the lobby, Velcro patches on their vests removed to reveal white letters claiming membership in SWAT. It was a convenient fiction, and they yelled and waved at the after-hours workers panicked by the alarms as they entered.

Sheen positioned herself behind the main desk and hit the controls to lock the elevators out of the top fifteen floors. Kettner moved like one experienced at evacuations, shouting orders and pushing people into exit lines on his way to the right side of the lobby and the freight elevator. Khan angled left toward the private lifts that served the highest levels.

Sheen connected the final cable to the computer behind the main desk and asked, "Are you in?"

Dornan replied, "Yep, full access. Opening the executive elevators. Summoning the freight elevator. It's on twenty-four."

Khan set the heavy case he carried down and dialed a code into the keypad on the side. Two rovers—the hounds—emerged and rolled toward the open doors of the nearby lifts. A pair of drones with cameras—Dornan called them her canaries—rose on spinning rotors from compartments built into the top. The device was a high-powered wireless signal booster that connected Dornan's toys to the city network, and thence to her.

"Ground team, time to…" Sheen paused, then finished in a sing-song voice, "get higher, baby." The three met at the far side of the lobby and headed for the freight elevator.

———

The math had been perfect. Binot's mind supplied the "as always" that Dornan would have added. Her momentum and the irresistible pull of gravity sent her on a pendulum arc toward the skyscraper, causing the harness' heavy ballistic fiber to dig into her flesh, guaranteeing bruises once the day's adventure was done.

Assuming, of course, that the WMW upstairs didn't create a fire spear and gut her with it. The world had some seriously strange shit in it these days, no doubt about that.

She had two choices as she swung toward the building, and both sucked. First, the perfect math would draw an arc that resulted in her slamming into the ceiling at full speed before falling to the floor, momentum spent. That would hurt, but it was a guaranteed entry.

The other option required her to detach the main cable at just the right instant to change her trajectory without missing the window, depositing her deeper in the level and eliminating the quick stop against the immovable object.

Hopefully also avoiding whatever else might be present in there.

She was still debating it when instinct took over and she pulled the release strap. Binot flew into the unleased space and smashed through a series of card tables and folding chairs before fetching up against a heavy tool cabinet, her helmet slamming into it hard enough to make her ears ring.

She staggered up, shaking her head, and found a support pillar to attach her backup line to. "Croft is in. Cable secure, Ninja."

After several moments, he ziplined into view. They slipped out of their harnesses and checked one another's gear. Everything was good.

"Just another day in the Corps," Parker quipped, gesturing her into the lead.

"I love the Corps. Every formation a parade, yadda yadda," she answered, striding toward the emergency stairwell. "Moving on up, Boss."

―――――

"Copy," Sheen replied. The trio stood atop the freight elevator as it climbed the spine of the building. The shaft was dusty and dark around them, even with the low-light augmentation of their goggles. Still, the roof was a far safer position than the cabin if something tried to stop them.

Naturally, shortly after she processed that thought, her luck ran out. The elevator shuddered to a halt.

"Saber?"

"Power is out in all the elevators. There must be a physical switch somewhere because the electronics all read right. The good news is that you should be able to force the doors. The bad news is that there are a bunch of heat signals on the floor below you. Is going the rest of the way up the shaft an option?"

Sheen looked up into the darkness and considered their options. "No. Too risky. No cover. We need to get out of here."

"Okay. Better bet is to go up one. Canary shows it empty."

"Got it. That we can do."

They jumped to the ladder that ran beside the doorway and climbed to the next level. She and Kettner supported Khan for several minutes as he worked the doors free. They released without warning, sending them stumbling out into the elevator's lobby.

"Okay, show me the stairs," Sheen ordered. The AR in her goggles drew a wireframe; the main staircase was at a sixty-degree angle from where they were, through the offices in front of them.

They crossed to the stairwell, leapfrogging from cover to cover in case the canary had missed something. They opened the door as Binot and Parker stumbled up the stairs, looking disheveled and adrenaline-spiked.

"What happened to you?" Sheen asked.

"Zombies," Parker panted. "Gods. Damned. Zombies."

"They're not really zombies," Binot replied, smacking her partner on the shoulder. "But they seem dumber than average and appear to be under some sort of compulsion, and they are way tougher than you'd expect them to be. Shots that would drop a human don't bother them. We had to shoot them in the legs a lot and run, and they crawled after us."

"Maybe I should take the lead," said Kettner, hoisting his automatic shotgun. "This baby will blow limbs right off. Perfect for humans, zombies, vampires, and whatever the hell else might be up there."

Parker looked at Binot, who looked at Sheen, who shrugged. "Be my guest, newbie. Don't die to impress us, though. We don't care how big your dick is; we just want you around to use it."

Kettner opened his mouth, then closed it. He opened it again, failed to find anything useful to do with it, and shook his head as he walked forward, shotgun at the ready. Sheen suppressed her laughter as she met Binot's eyes. Hazing the new recruits was one of the things that made life worth living. Of course, once he learned that she took it as well as she gave it, she expected the Army officer to send some choice comments her way in return.

The team followed, Khan in the center, Binot on rear guard. Parker stayed three feet behind their point man, his rifle traversing in a careful pattern, up right, up middle, up left, middle left, an arc to avoid pointing it at his ally's back, middle right, and up to begin the sequence again. The rhythm was calming.

The only sounds in the stairwell were their footsteps. At the fifty-first floor, Sheen started to get nervous. When they reached sixty without contact, the nerves had transformed into a certainty that something bad was imminent. It therefore wasn't as big a shock as it should have been when the doors slammed open on the three floors below them and a flock of enemies appeared, swords in hand.

"Faster," Binot said, her voice rising as she spoke. "Faster." Her rifle chattered. "Must move faster. Go, go, go!"

The team burst out of the stairwell onto the top floor with an army of foot soldiers behind them. As soon as they were through, Binot latched the door and Khan trapped it with explosives while the others fanned out to secure the space. It was filled with shadow, as if the spell that had transformed the windows had also caused them to absorb and dissipate the light.

It was an empty and hopeless place. Sheen felt dark magic all around. She reached deep within, tapping the well of potential that rested there, and cast both arms out wide. Tattoos glowed on her hands, joining the scarlet Eye of Horus that was always there, hidden behind her watch face; always vigilant, always protecting her.

Her power swept out and shattered the illusion that blinded them. Triple their number of enemies appeared, again with swords, arrayed in matching rows in reducing numbers before the central feature of the large empty space. He sat in a double-sized leather chair, a virtual giant of a man who topped seven feet. His muscles were bulky; huge, but conveying a sense of strain as if they struggled to hold in the raw intensity of his being.

Soft gold eyes caught their attention and urged trust and submission. They were set in an almost angelic face, with a light beard caressing his jaw and reaching up to touch his thin mustache. Luxurious hair cascaded over his shoulders onto the button-down shirt he wore. Sheen took in the rest of him and snorted.

"Business-casual demon. That's something new."

His eyes narrowed, and several of his minions twitched. He raised a hand, and the movement stopped. "Greetings, mortals. I am the Fallen. You may address me as 'Master.' Thank you for responding to my invitation."

Binot stepped beside Sheen, hands positioned on the rifle that rested on her chest. "I knew this seemed too easy."

The giant being laughed. "Indeed. Had I wished you stopped, stopped you would have been. But, no; I have been waiting for you, Agent Diana Sheen, and you, Agent Franklin Kettner. You will help me enter the place where you hold my subjects, and you will help me free them."

Kettner's laugh was hoarse and short. "I think I speak for both of us when I say there's no fucking chance we're doing that, you sack of demonic dirt."

Sheen nodded. "What he said goes double for me, douchenugget. You'll get to visit your buddies in the Cube all right, but you're gonna be staying for a while. A long while. I suggest you come quietly." She added a shrug that suggested she didn't care if he came quietly or not and might actually prefer the latter.

His expansive grin showed his teeth. They were all pointed, and some appeared too wicked to fit in his mouth. As he stood and unfolded to his full height, the room seemed to strain to accommodate him. His laughter blended mockery and genuine amusement. "You will have an eternity in my service to make up for your insolence, Agent Diana Sheen." He made an intricate gesture with his arms, and sibilant sounds hissed forth. His minions shuddered from stillness into life, from guarding to readiness to attack. They shook like horses held back from a gallop until his command released them.

"Sheen and Kettner are mine. Kill the rest." They screamed in pleasure and charged.

Kettner's shotgun barked and one in the front rank fell to the ground, but they were fast—too fast—and closed before projectiles could eliminate many. Binot, Khan, and Parker spread out with no need for words, firing pistols as they moved to put their backs against separate walls. The explosives-rigged door to the stairwell opened, and claymores detonated to shred the minions trying to climb up and join the fight.

Sheen charged the Fallen, the pistol in her right hand barking as she flicked the baton to full extension with her left. She crossed Kettner's line of fire, so he pulled the shotgun from its sling and ran in, the barrel warm even through his gloves as he swung the stock at the giant's neck.

With a sweeping blow, the giant knocked the weapons out of Sheen's hands and sent her rolling, to crash into a column half the room away. She arched in pain and writhed as she fought to breathe. The attack continued into a kick that separated Kettner from his improvised club and dropped him flat on his back. He bounced to his feet and ran to Sheen, pulling her up.

She griped in a hoarse voice as she found her balance, "He hits like a truck. Not a small truck. Like, a big truck. Like, the biggest truck."

"He must be augmenting his strength with his magic somehow, the buff bastard. Or he just really, really likes the gym."

"I'm sure he's got more tricks to show us, but it's too risky to draw them out. Ninja, Croft, Glam, you ready?"

"Gods, yes. Playing with these idiots is boring," Binot replied, followed by a series of creative curses aimed at another of the minions.

"All right, then. Phase two. Execute."

The team members had been chosen for their magic potential in addition to their other skills. Rigorous training had taught each a set of useful combat spells. As one, the trio cast a force barrier to throw their opponents back, hurling them away and knocking several to the floor. Blanchett shouted the words of an incantation to negate the Fallen's magical hold on them and render them either inert or free-willed, but it failed to stop them from struggling to their feet. Parker shrugged and put a double-tap into the head of the nearest, ensuring he would not rise again.

Pistols barked, and their enemies stayed down, dead or damaged enough they couldn't continue. Binot left the other two to finish the cleanup and charged at the Fallen, her gun clicking empty as she sent rounds at him. She flicked the magazine release and reached for a replacement, then threw herself into a dive, her helmet cracking on the floor. The move barely saved her from the spear of fire the demon had hurled, which impacted and disintegrated behind her, sending a wash of flame in every direction. She rolled to smother any that had caught her and leapt up with a growl to press the attack.

Before she could get there, a series of metal panels fell from the ceiling, creating an impenetrable barrier separating them from the demon and their people. Binot screamed in frustration and turned to run for the stairwell, hoping that the level below wasn't filled with more minions, calling for Khan and Parker to follow.

Sheen and Kettner circled the Fallen, radiating light as they launched magical attacks. Sheen's magic was indirect, brilliant tendrils swirling from her outstretched hands as they sought an opening. They burned where they touched, covering him in small but wicked wounds. Kettner's approach was more direct. He pressed his palms together, and when he pulled them apart, an orb of white light appeared. A squeeze flattened it into a disc. He created and threw them in a blur of motion, some straight, some with enough English on them to impress a professional frisbee-golfer.

The Fallen received long slashes from the discs to complement the wasp stings of the tendrils as he fought the dual onslaught. Kettner and Sheen stayed on the move and remained far apart, ensuring a single strike couldn't get them both. The demon created shields to hide behind and intercepted the discs he couldn't block with orbs of dark power that shattered them. He fired more of the spheres at the two agents, forcing them to dodge and slowing the attacks just enough to marshal his focus. With a bellow, he clenched his fists and threw his arms into the air, hurling a blast of visible darkness through the space.

Kettner and Sheen summoned shields, but the wave 's force was irresistible. They slid, pushing against its weight, boots fighting for a grip on the smooth floor. When the storm ended the Fallen stood tall, his clothes torn and punctured but a wide smile on his face. "Good, you have power. You will be excellent additions to my army." He reached out with an open palm as if inviting them to join him and murmured an invocation. A flaming pillar erupted, reaching to the ceiling. He caressed the blaze with his other hand, both arms now aglow with orange-red tattoos that burned away the cloth covering them. When his manipulations were through, he held a sword made of fire.

"They will damage you, but I will heal you, and through healing, make you my own," he promised. The blade sliced through the tendrils and deflected discs as he strode toward Kettner.

"Boss, this isn't looking so good," Kettner said. He rolled to the side to avoid a strike that would have taken out one of his legs.

"Keep him occupied. He seems to like you. Maybe we can turn this into a honeytrap." He snorted in response, and she continued, "Croft, status."

"Thirty seconds," Binot panted. Sheen nodded and rushed at the Fallen. His spine was to her as he pursued Kettner, and she readied herself for a leaping kick to his head. In an instant, though, he had turned, faster than she could follow, and his sword whipped across at chest level. The jump became a slide, and the heat from the confined fire blistered her cheek as it crossed an inch from her eye. She chambered her leg and pistoned it out, connecting with the side of his knee and collapsing it.

As he fell toward his failed joint, Kettner snapped a constant stream of flattened orbs at his face. He interposed the sword and punched down with his other hand, but Sheen evaded and rolled until she gained enough space to get to her feet. She thrust out her hands, and tentacles erupted again, each one seeking his eyes from a different angle. When he adjusted the flaming blade to block them, discs struck him, the repeated force staggering him as he rose. Again, he bellowed and threw his arms up, and another wave of power washed over them. Sheen conjured a shield and held firm against the blast.

The door to the stairwell banged open and her team emerged, firing as they neared. Darts of light erupted from Binot's fingers, finding holes in his defenses as he fought to block both tentacles and discs, drawing yelps and angry screams. Parker went with a tried-and-true tactic, aiming triple bursts at the Fallen's legs. Khan targeted the arm that held the fire sword with his rifle. The agents were silent, only breathing and grunts of exertion filling the comm. Now that they were reunited, doubt had fled, leaving only coordinated discipline in its wake.

The barrage brought the giant to one knee, then to both, and his weapon flickered and died. With a gesture he caused the metal barrier to retract, allowing his minions access, but the few who remained could do no more than crawl. He hung his head, defeated.

"It's so sad to see how far he's fallen," quipped Binot. The rest of the team groaned. Sheen smacked her on the arm.

"That was incredibly dumb. You just earned yourself the job of dragging him down to the ground floor."

"Can I throw him out a window?"

Sheen thought about it for a second, then shook her head. "No, I think we'll need him in better shape than that. I'm guessing the idiot has information we or the Oriceran consulate could use." Parker and Khan bound the demon's arms and legs and shoved a gag in his mouth so he couldn't cast.

The elevators opened. Dornan sounded happy as she asked, "Want a ride?" The team moved to accept the offer.

Binot alone chose a different path and pulled the Fallen by a line tied around his feet toward the door. "We'll take the stairs. Meet you at the bottom."

As the doors closed, they could hear the thuds as she dragged him down the steps behind her, sixty-three floors' worth awaiting him.

The women again sat across the elegant glass desk from one another. Both sported bandages and radiated weariness in their slumped postures. The transfer of the Fallen to the Cube had required hours of attention and effort. Sheen stared at Binot in silence, waiting.

The blonde coughed in faux apology. "So, as I was saying, we need more people. And more magic."

"Funny you should say that. A message from the oversight committee arrived while we were dropping off the scumbag."

"And?"

"Apparently the Fallen is a bigger threat than the Oricerans thought at first, so we've got approval to bring on a couple more field agents and a boatload of support personnel."

"That's not enough."

Sheen glared at her but winced as the bandage across her

burned cheek pulled. "Dammit, Cara, are you still here whining? Get the fuck out and find us some people to put in harm's way."

Binot stood and strode to the door, but turned before leaving. "Boss?"

A long, drawn-out sigh. "Yes?"

"Next time, maybe stay on the bus." Binot tried and failed to smother a smirk.

"Bite me, Croft."

She laughed as she fled the office.

AUTHOR NOTES

Written November 12, 2018

Thank you for reading this story. I hope you enjoyed reading it as much as I enjoyed writing it!

I've just returned from the soul-nurturing 20booksto50k conference in Las Vegas, where I got to revel in the companion-ship and positive energy of 700+ indie authors.

It's amazing that such an industry exists. I am grateful every day to be a part of it.

This is my first foray into Urban Fantasy, although it carries some of the themes from my Military Science Fiction stories—an ensemble cast, strong characters who face challenges and grow, and the sort of snarky dialogue I'd love to have in my workplace! I'm a big fan of Dresden, of course.

The Oriceran universe is great fun to read and write in. When I first read Martha Carr's books, but before I read Brownstone, I knew exactly what I was going to write. A bounty hunter who tracked down creatures from the other world! Such a freaking awesome idea!

Turns out someone else thought it was a great idea before I

did and delivered bigtime, so Diane Sheen and the Agency were born!

If you enjoyed the story and want to let me know about it, you can find me on Facebook at https://www.facebook.com/AuthorTRCameron or via email at thom@trcameron.com. If you have thoughts on improving it, same addresses!

Thank you again for reading! Wishing you joys upon joys – so may it be.

—TR

TROLL TALES

BY MANDI F

What happens when mischievous, fun-loving trolls get caught up in something bigger than themselves? When things are a-changin' and mysterious goings-on are afoot, follow this determined and adventurous trio to the answers they seek.

We all know what curiosity did to the cat, but who can help themselves when it seems like it's the right...well, really, the *only* thing to do?

To Tom, my ever patient and supportive husband who introduced me to the LMBPN Universe and to all the Fuzzys in the world, who are told they are obstinate and headstrong, but truly believe they have no other choice but to do what they believe is the right thing.

TROLL TALES

Why is everything so dark? Why can't I see?

Trying to open my eyes seems like too much work right now. Maybe I'll try again later.

Or I'll try again now, Fuzzy thought when she realized something wasn't right.

My head hurts, and I can't see. What the hell?

Panic started to creep in.

Something was seriously wrong, but I just can't remember what. It seems like I should remember; that I should know why I can't see, and why my head hurts like hell. Why can't I remember?

Breathing deeply in an attempt to calm down before her panic became full-blown and took on a life of its own, Fuzzy concentrated on the last things she *could* remember.

Fun. Excitement. A surprise. Family. Celebration.

"That's great," Fuzzy muttered to herself. "As usual, it's all feelings and no details."

For as long as she could remember, Fuzzy's empathy had been off the scale, but she didn't know how to be any different. Everyone she came across made her feel so deeply.

At first, her family hadn't thought it was such a big deal since once trolls bonded, they focused on the emotions of whoever they were bonded with. They were very proud that she was so bright and showing such great promise at an early age, but when her emotions started overwhelming her regularly, she could feel their worry and concern.

She felt everything deep in her soul, everything everyone around her felt—the joy, the happiness, the kindness, the confidence, the sadness, the jealousy, the irritability, the anxiety, the anger. Everything, good and bad.

Sometimes she had to shut down for her own sanity. She had found that spending time alone was the only way she was able to ground herself. A clearing deep in the Dark Forest had become one of her favorite places to relax and reconnect to her own feelings.

Is that where I am? Am I in the Dark Forest? Fuzzy thought as hard as she could, but still drew a blank. She had no idea where she was and why her head hurt like hell, and it still seemed like way too much effort to open her eyes. *Maybe a short nap will help. Deep breathing to try to relax, maybe just a short nap. Get your strength back, then everything will get figured out.*

Orville continued pacing outside the Healing Center, waiting for a report of any change in Fuzzy's condition so he could update Pearl.

He couldn't believe this had happened to Fuzzy. She, Pearl, and Orville had always been best friends. Fuzzy led the way, Pearl looked after everyone, and he was happy to follow them anywhere. He always knew what he should do by following their lead. Now he felt lost, like a part of him was missing and he didn't know how to find it again.

The Senior Healer had told him over and over that Fuzzy would wake up when she was ready. Her body and mind needed to heal; then she would wake on her own. There was nothing they could do to help; it was all up to her.

Pearl came screeching around the corner of the building, completely out of breath and holding something in her arms like her life depended on it.

"What the hell, Pearl?" asked a puzzled Orville, "There's been no change. They thought she was waking up a little while ago, but no such luck."

"But, but, but…" Pearl huffed and puffed, trying to get her breath back. "I felt her coming around from the herb garden on the other side of the village. I know it was her; she was so confused and scared. I grabbed every healing herb I could find and came racing over here to help her."

"You know they won't let us in before she wakes up," Orville replied kindly. "We've been told in no uncertain terms that if we make ourselves a nuisance, they won't even let me wait out here."

"She needs us, Orville; I can feel it. She doesn't understand what's gone on. She's in pain, and she can't figure out how to wake up. She's confused and frightened. Maybe if I speak with the Senior Healer, he'll let us in, if only for a little while?" Pearl suggested hopefully.

Given Pearl's misery and Fuzzy's pain, he agreed to approach the Senior Healer again. He crossed his fingers, hoping the healer didn't chase them out again and find something else for them to do rather than getting under his feet.

Orville approached the Healing Center with trepidation, looking around the doors cautiously to find the Senior Healer. He almost jumped out of his skin as a small voice to his right asked him if he was okay. After the beating of his heart slowed to an acceptable level, he recognized Bloom, the Relief Healer, poking her head around an office door.

Seeing Bloom there, Orville's hope that they could get in to see Fuzzy grew.

Bloom queried again, "Are you okay, Orville? Do you need anything?"

"We'd really like to see Fuzzy. Pearl felt her trying to wake up from across the village. I know it isn't the way things are usually done, but Pearl really thinks she can help. You know she's really good with the gardens and helps things grow and get better. I don't know how she could hear Fuzzy all the way over there since I was just outside and didn't hear anything, but she swore that it happened. And maybe it did, like when we both heard Fuzzy when she was hurt, but please, please, please don't send us away. Please let us see her, if only for a little while. We promise not to get in the way. We will leave as soon as you say we must, but we need to see her. Maybe it will help, and..." Orville babbled, saying anything and everything that came into his head, hoping it that might help get both in to see their friend. Even if Bloom said no, he'd given it his best shot.

"Since Fuzzy is currently the only patient in the Healing Center and she's in stable condition, the Senior Healer has gone home for a few hours to rest," Bloom explained to a hopeful Orville. "As long as you can be quiet and there's no messing around, you can come in and talk to her for a little while. Talking might help, especially if Pearl felt her from the other side of the village."

"Thank you, thank you, thank you," Orville whispered as he ran out the door to get Pearl.

As I dozed, I could feel worry and deep concern from someone close. Well, more than one someone. I needed to get up to see what was wrong. It wasn't the first time I'd been woken from sleep by someone else's feelings that I couldn't just turn off, but it seemed so immediate and urgent that I needed to try to help right now.

Once I finally got them open, I blinked my eyes slowly to accustom myself to the light in the room. I realized I wasn't home in my own cozy bed, but somewhere else. The pain in my head brought it all back. Well, some of it back.

Pearl gasped, pushed Orville out of the room to go get Bloom, and rushed to Fuzzy's side, murmuring, "Everything's all right. Everything's going to be okay now that you're awake."

"What the hell? What's happened? Where am I? Why does my head hurt so much?"

"There was an accident," Pearl explained soothingly, "*You* had an accident. We've been so worried. You weren't waking up; you've been asleep for two days. But now that you're awake, everything will be okay. You'll be fine, I just know it."

"What happened?"

"We were hoping you could tell us the answer to that question," commented Bloom as she walked into the room to check Fuzzy's vitals. "What was the last thing you remember?"

"Fun, excitement, a surprise, family, celebration, but no detail. I don't know why or who?" Fuzzy replied.

"Of course, you'd remember that," Pearl gushed with excitement, "Yumfuck came home to visit, and he brought Earth-style magical food. We all had Cheetos and Twinkies and Doritos. It was wonderful to see him, and we had an enormous celebration. Although now I think about it, I didn't see you later on. Did you go on one of your walks?"

"I sort of remember. It's not very clear, like something is interfering with my memory of that night. When I try to think back, it all goes kind of hazy and confusing." Fuzzy mused, trying to work out what had happened.

Looking at the three young trolls, Bloom sighed. She knew that Fuzzy needed more rest but was also aware that the three of them were as thick as thieves. If she wanted to keep Fuzzy here for a few more days of observation, the other two would be here as well. Might as well let them catch up before the

Senior Healer came back in and set down his rules with an iron rod.

Reminding them that Fuzzy needed as much rest as possible and not to overdo, Bloom went back to her office. Although Fuzzy's vitals had all been normal, she'd noticed a small bruise on the back of her head that looked new but didn't seem painful. Bloom noted it in Fuzzy's chart and didn't think much more about it.

The sun was shining the day Fuzzy finally left the Healing Center. She wasn't the most patient of trolls and kept wanting to get up and help others, but when the Senior Healer threatened seriously to keep her even longer if she didn't rest, resting it was. And really, she did feel much better after the extra couple of days of bed rest, although her memories still hadn't come back.

As she walked out of the Healing Center into the middle of the village, she stopped for a moment. Trolls were everywhere, playing and rolling around in the grass, laughing and trilling. Wonderful carved wooden houses as far as she could see. So awesome to see everyone so happy and normal; just what she craved after the isolation of the Healing Center.

Orville and Pearl had walked over to help celebrate her release day. They looked great together and would be a perfect match if only they both realized it.

Pearl was so beautiful with her lush silver tuft, and amazingly graceful. Being the patient and caring troll she was, she just adored her garden and it adored her back. All trolls had sensational horticultural skills, but Pearl's were completely off the charts. Fuzzy was sure she talked to her plants and knew what they needed before they did. She was famous throughout Oriceran for her healing herbs, with customers from Rodania to the Kingdom of Virgo, and she was even starting to get a few customers from kemanas on Earth.

Orville was the perfect complement to Pearl, friendly and helpful with a heart of gold. He might not be as flashy as some of the other trolls, with a brown tuft that was almost the same color as the rest of him, but he was the most supportive, happy troll Fuzzy had ever met. And really, that was saying something, considering trolls were generally happy.

Fuzzy thought, *They've always both been there for me. Even when I grew into my 'gift' and it started causing problems. They never left me, always understood, or if they didn't understand, supported me anyway. I love them both so much, and I'm proud to be able to call them friends.*

"But I need to know!"

Orville knew that when Fuzzy became this determined, arguing with her wouldn't change her mind. She never let a question or mystery go. She needed answers to all the questions, even the ones no one else thought to ask. He had always admired her and loved her deeply as one of his best friends. Her adventurous ways just weren't for him, although he always seemed to find himself going along, if only to try to keep her out of as much trouble as possible. He would never forgive himself if something bad happened to her and he wasn't there to help. And now she had another mystery to unravel.

"Have you remembered any more of the day Yumfuck visited?" Pearl asked. She wanted to be supportive, but as Fuzzy started to feel better, she hoped that they could move on and not go looking for trouble. But really, she wouldn't be Fuzzy if she didn't follow her heart, and Fuzzy's huge heart needed to explore and discover the answers.

Fuzzy went silent for a moment, then admitted with a sigh, "It was all just too much. I loved seeing Yumfuck and was happy to have him visit with his magical foods from Earth, but it was all just too much. The euphoria was hurting my head. I could feel everything from everyone, and I needed quiet for a little while."

"I walked into the Dark Forest for a little peace and quiet and felt something else—overwhelming fear and panic. I didn't even think, I just ran toward it to see if there was anything I could do."

Orville gasped in horror. "You ran *toward* it? You didn't think to run back to the village for help? *You ran toward it?* What have I told you? I will always be there for you. Don't go toward the bad stuff without me!"

"Well, I didn't know what it was, so I had to go and see if I could help. If I had come back to the village, I might have been too late," Fuzzy tried to explain.

Pearl just rolled her eyes. Of course, Fuzzy would run to help with no thought to her own safety, just the safety of others.

"Do you remember which way you went?" Pearl asked quietly, trying to keep the peace. There really wasn't anything they could do now about Fuzzy's having run off, but she thought she'd have a good "talk" with her later about how to maybe do things a bit better and safer in the future.

Walking slowly toward the edge of the village, Fuzzy looked around like she was hearing something. With a strange look on her face, she continued stepping forward slowly like she could still hear whatever she had followed days ago. But she *couldn't* still hear it, could she?

As she and her friends traveled farther into the Dark Forest, the peace and serenity that usually soothed her in there were missing. It was like there was an echo of the fear and panic she'd felt, and somehow she could still follow it. She needed to find its source and figure out what the hell had happened.

Fuzzy worked through the confusing emotions in her mind as they followed the echo that only she could hear. She realized that she didn't even know how she had gotten back to the village that fateful day. How had she ended up in the Healing Center?

"Just after Yumfuck left, we felt you. You were projecting panic and fear, but we didn't know where you were. The whole village started a search and you were found not long after, unconscious by a large old tree that appeared to have scorch marks on it. We didn't think any more about it then. Our obvious priority was to get you back to the Healing Center," Orville explained.

"Then let's get to that tree and see what we can find out."

Although the usual feeling of contentment didn't come, it did make her feel a little better to have a plan of action to try to work out what went on. Why did her head still hurt, and why didn't she quite feel herself? She was sure memory loss wasn't a great indicator that she was well. The Senior Healer had said it could take a few days to be back to normal, but she might never get the memories of that day back.

Anyone who knew her well knew that she would find that completely unacceptable. She would get those memories back, no matter what. She needed to find out what had happened to her, and she had a feeling she had to do something else. Something important. She just needed to remember what it is.

She'd always enjoyed spending time in the Dark Forest, not just for the peace and serenity, but also the wild beauty of the dense and ancient trees. Yes, there were certain places they had been warned about going as little ones, but she'd never felt threatened or anything. Even the stories about the Gardener didn't scare her, although she'd never met him. She felt a sense of safety about him. Strange, really; that felt new. Although he had moved to the Sanctuary on Earth, somehow she knew his spirit was still in their forest, ready to summon him if necessary. She wondered if he knew what had happened?

As they got closer to the large old tree she was found next to, they all stared in awe. It was magnificent. Towering hundreds of feet into the sky, its beautiful canopy was full of birds singing the most beautiful songs.

And something else. Something else was up there, she could tell. It wasn't threatening the birds or they wouldn't be singing, but Fuzzy could feel it. And she'd felt it before. It felt different, like it was not in its place. It felt almost alien.

Fuzzy's body tensed, making her fur stand on end. Pearl and Orville looked at her curiously, unsure what was upsetting her.

"Is it being in this place? We don't have to stay, you know. We can just go home. Maybe you need some more rest?" Orville asked hopefully.

"Can you not feel it?" Fuzzy exclaimed. "Something different? Something not meant to be here?"

Pearl tried to calm Fuzzy down. "We can feel that you're upset —somehow you're doing that projecting thing again, so we feel what you're feeling—but we can't feel anything else."

"Trust me, something's here; I can feel it. It's different, and it doesn't belong here. It's scared and doesn't know what to do. We need to help it."

"How do we help if you don't know what it is or what it wants?" Orville asked, "If it's all the way up in the canopy, how can we get it to come down? It's not like we can just ask it to."

All of a sudden Fuzzy started to grow, her concern for whatever was scared and alone in the canopy forcing her to get taller and taller. She started to smell something strange, like patchouli and wet dog. It smelled like a silver bear. How could that be? What the hell?

Fuzzy wanted to back away from the tree as fast as she could since even *she* knew not to go toward a silver bear, but there was something in the sad, scared feelings that drew her. Somehow she knew the silver bear wouldn't hurt her; that it was lost and terrified. As she got closer, she saw multiple shimmering visions of a very young silver bear that was gripping the branches tightly in its panic.

Despite Fuzzy not knowing how her projecting thing worked, she tried to send out soothing thoughts and feelings to the cub to calm it down. The projections the cub had been flashing in defense started to fade and Fuzzy zoned in on the very tired bear, who thankfully crawled into her arms without much hesitation.

It was only then that Fuzzy realized how much she had grown. She looked down, then shut her eyes, pulled the bear cub close to her chest, and shrank back down to her usual size, with the bear cub holding onto her for dear life.

"Seriously, what the hell, Fuzzy? You *do* realize you just grew to a humungous size, *and* you brought a silver bear back with you? How the hell did you do that?" Pearl exclaimed. Orville just stood there with his mouth wide open and eyeballs almost falling out of his head.

"I have no idea. I didn't know I could do that. I just knew I needed to get to this little one. He's been up there for days all by himself, and I could feel how absolutely terrified he was," Fuzzy explained.

"Uhhh, so what are we going to do with him now?" asked Orville, "I'm not sure a troll village is the best place for him."

"I know, I know, but it's not like we can just leave him here. For a start, he won't let go of me. And really, how did he get here in the first place? He doesn't belong here. He's used to wide open spaces with plenty of room to roam, not the Dark Forest. He's too young to be away from his family; he can't look after himself yet. We have to look for his family."

Pearl and Orville glanced at each other, but they knew better than to argue, especially since they kind of agreed with what Fuzzy was saying. They weren't sure that adding another mystery to their lives right now would be very helpful, though.

"While you were growing up to the canopy, we found this scorch mark next to the tree, and it looks recent. Have you seen it before?" Orville asked, directing Fuzzy's attention to the scorch mark. It looked fresh. Fuzzy had been to this part of the forest many times and she'd never seen it, although it did remind her of something.

Pearl piped up with, "I know what that is; it's from a portal. Why would there be a portal all this way into the Dark Forest? It's not like there's anything here to see or do, other than lots of trees, of course."

As soon as Fuzzy approached the scorch mark, she felt strange. It was like there were echoes of something here; reverberations of pain and fear and anger. Was this a memory or something else? The silver bear cub whimpered louder the closer they got to the mark, and then he tried to dig into it, wailing. Fuzzy gave him a hug to try to soothe him, but although he stopped wailing, he clung to her and whimpered until he fell asleep.

Fuzzy's heart was breaking for this little guy, but until they worked out what all this meant, she wasn't sure how to help him. He needed his family, but she had no idea where to find them or even what had happened. As she turned to walk away from the tree, she tripped over an exposed root and the flashbacks started.

Screeching, pain, panic, roaring; a portal. It was open; there was fighting, so she ran into the middle of it, of course! She really needed to think this running into danger thing through in future!

There were elves and the silver bear cub and a large silver male—his dad—and something else. Something dark. It was trying to pull the silver bears through the portal and the elves were trying to stop it, she thought.

She shouted and distracted the dark thing long enough for the elves to get the upper hand, and they vanquished it, or most of it, at least. Something dark and shadow-like raced off into the Forest. The elves took off after it, leaving Fuzzy there with the two silver bears and an open portal.

Now that the immediate danger had passed, the silver bear cub, with the intense curiosity of the very young, reached out his paw to the shim-

mering portal and something latched onto him. He wailed in terror and tried to pull his paw back, but it wouldn't let go.

His dad roared and ripped into the portal with his sharp claws, trying desperately to get his son, but whatever it was, it didn't let go. All claws and ferocious teeth, the cub's dad jumped into the portal, forcing the thing to let go of his son...and the portal snapped shut.

The silver bear cub and Fuzzy looked at each other and...

Black.

———

After Fuzzy told the others what she had remembered, they all sat there a while and stared at each other, unsure what to do next.

There was some sort of black shadow thing roaming the Dark Forest, something equally scary living in portals, a missing silver bear, and a silver bear cub that needed looking after. What was with her projection of emotions? The weird lump on the back of her head? And oh, she had grown so tall she was up in the forest canopy. That wasn't normal, even for her!

Their discussions went around and around, but they couldn't work anything out. Things just seemed too strange. The cub started to stir, and all Fuzzy wanted to do was make him happy and give him the life he deserved after being stranded in the canopy of the Dark Forest for the last four days and having to watch his father ripped away from him into a portal to who knew where.

Suddenly there was crackling, and a portal opened right in front of them. They all jumped up and moved away, very aware of what had happened to the silver bear cub so recently.

As the portal steadied, out walked the mythic Gardener of the Dark Forest, holding his twisted vine staff. After eyeing them, he stepped over to the silver bear cub and gently picked him up, cooing soothingly to him the whole time.

"Um, sir?" Fuzzy stuttered, trying to explain. "We didn't hurt him. We found him here, scared and alone, and just wanted to help."

"You've done well, young trolls," the Gardener began. "I know you only had his best interests at heart. I could feel it from Earth and followed your love and concern here. I must be going since I have a very anxious father in my Sanctuary, waiting eagerly to reunite with this young one. But before I leave, let me give you a piece of advice: please be careful in the Dark Forest at this time. There are strange things running around, and not all have goodness in their hearts like you do. I believe we will meet again in the not-too-distant future. Until then, take care."

To say all three trolls were surprised would be an understatement. Stories of the Gardener of the Dark Forest and his fierce protection of his wildlife were rampant, but they had never thought they would actually see or meet him. Fuzzy felt his warmth and watchfulness, as well as a sense of pride in the trolls and something else. What, she wasn't sure, but there was something behind his eyes that told her he knew more than he was saying.

As the portal closed behind the Gardener and the silver bear cub, the trio started back to the village. Not everything had been answered to their satisfaction, and dangerous and confusing things were afoot in the Dark Forest, but at least the little silver bear would be with his father tonight, so all was good in his world.

Fuzzy wanted to know more about her new abilities. If she could project all the way to the Gardener on Earth well enough for him to follow the projection back to her, she needed to be careful about what she was doing. Although it was a good thing, wasn't it?

Also, what about the ability to grow enormous? She'd only heard of trolls being able to do that once they were bonded to others, and she wasn't bonded, was she? She couldn't be bonded and not know about it, could she?

It would be exciting to go off and see more of the universe, maybe even Earth. The Gardener had said that they would meet again. She wondered when that would be.

Those were more than enough questions for her first day out and about from the Healing Center. She was tired now, and a nap in her own bed sounded like a wonderful idea, but she felt wonderful about doing a good deed for the silver bear cub and finding out what had happened to her. Or was there more to know? They all knew what curiosity did to the cat, but sometimes she just couldn't help herself.

After Orville and Pearl dropped Fuzzy off at home, they exchanged a look. That knowing look, the one that said they knew Fuzzy wouldn't be down for long. They expected to delve into more mysteries in the near future because wherever Fuzzy led, they'd follow.

If only to keep her safe from herself.

AUTHOR'S NOTES

Thank you, thank you, thank you.

To you the reader, who thought this was entertaining enough to read, to Martha Carr for working so hard her whole life to get to the point where she created this Universe, to Michael Anderle for helping to create this Universe and providing this opportunity for aspiring writers all over the world. To everyone who has supported, cajoled, and encouraged the new writers, and the not so new.

This is something I've always wanted to do, but I've never been sure it would be possible.

My very supportive husband has listened to me speak for many long hours about my dreams and wishes on this subject and has been subtly (or not so subtly) pushing me to sit down and get the damn thing done for a long time. Here it is.

Thank you to everyone,
Mandi

ALL IN A DAY'S WORK

BY LISA FRETT

Stephanie and Trig are in a hurry to find and stop a psychotic and murderous gnome.

The gnome Pembroke is tired of working for the Light Elves in their library on Oriceran. He finally has what he needs to leave his misery behind and bring his own form of misery to the planet Earth.

Will Stephanie and Trig find him in time? Or will the humans of northern Vermont be in danger from the murderous little bugger?

With the help of two child ogres, the witch Stephanie and her wizard partner Trig must find and stop psycho-gnome Pembroke before he turns northern Vermont into his killing ground.

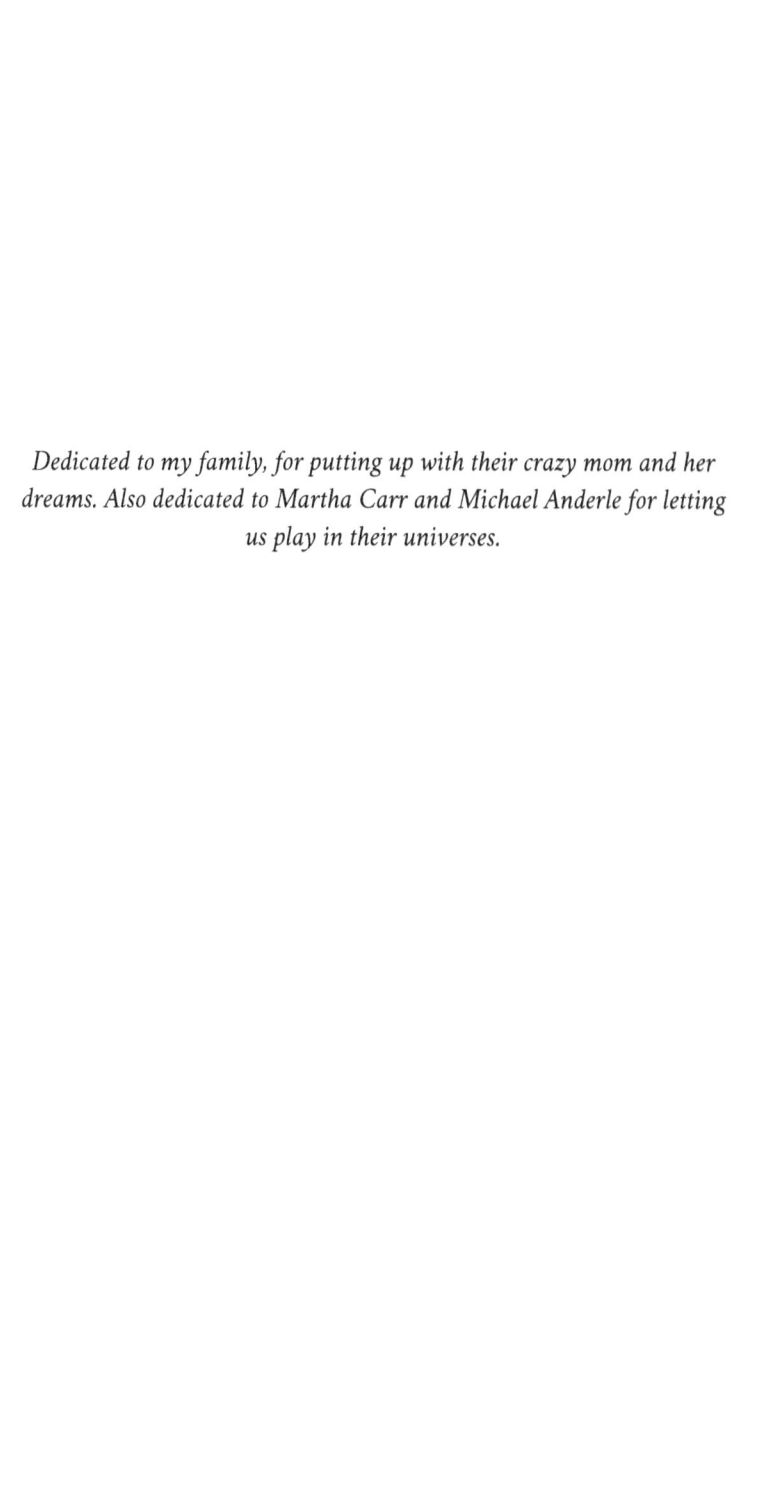

Dedicated to my family, for putting up with their crazy mom and her dreams. Also dedicated to Martha Carr and Michael Anderle for letting us play in their universes.

PROLOGUE

The bitter gnome kicked the corpse of the dead elf at his feet. "Stupid elf," he said aloud. "You all think you're better than the rest of us. Well, you're not!" He kicked the body again and spat on it.

He grimaced as he wiped off his daggers on the dead elf's shirt.

The murderous gnome, Pembroke, looked down at his once-clean suit. There was blood all over his clothes. *It's just as well*, he thought. *Once I leave Oriceran, I won't have to wear these stupid suits anymore anyway.*

As a gnome working in the Light Elves' library, it was required that he wear a suit and a bowler hat. The suit itched like mad, and it made him miserable. The bowler hat they gave him was too small for his head and made his ears poke out. All you could see of his face were his big ears and his huge nose with a hairy little wart on its tip. There was an evil little poppy flower on the hat band that had a mouth with sharp teeth that tried to bite his fingers whenever he held the hat in his hands.

The flower on his hat was meant to be an alarm of sorts, one that would warn the wearer of any danger to the library and its books. All Pembroke's hat flower did was terrorize him. He wished that the little flower would wilt and die.

Pembroke glanced at the corpse. *Arrogant, self-righteous snob of an elf*, he thought. *That stupid elf believed that I would actually pay for the amulet?* "Bah!" he said aloud as he kicked the dead elf's corpse.

"I did all the hard work! All the research that went into the creation of these items, it was all me!" He kicked the corpse yet again. Apparently, he had anger issues.

Because of his position at the library, Pembroke had access to the rarest books, research, and documents on Oriceran. He had spent years researching a way to leave the godsforsaken planet. With the help of the now-dead elf wizard, he had been able to create magical items that would aid him in his quest to leave Oriceran for Earth.

Looking over the items that he created and that the Light Elf had spelled for him, he was overcome by the fact that he was finally ready to achieve his goal—to head for Earth, the planet where magic was unknown in most circles and illegal in all others. It would be his haven. The gnome hated books, and he hated the library. He hated Light Elves. He hated magic. Most of all, he hated Oriceran.

Pembroke picked up the first item, an amulet the shape of a disk. It looked like a planet with continents and water. On one side there was a map of the Earth's western hemisphere, and on the other was Oriceran's western hemisphere. The shape of the amulet was symbolic of its magic, that of opening a portal between Oriceran and Earth. Objects like this were relatively common on the black market, but he had made this one specifically for this moment. The fact that he created it made the item more personal.

The next item was a medallion. This one was a silver disk with the image of a human on it. The medallion was charmed so that when he wore it, non-magical beings would see a human.

Magical beings were immune to its spell, but that wouldn't be a problem once he made it to Earth. He just couldn't have humans see that he was a gnome. It was his understanding that gnomes didn't exist on Earth, so he couldn't be seen for what he was.

The last item was Pembroke's pride and joy. During his research on magical items and spells, he had found an obscure document that had mentioned a spell that could remove magic from items, and presumably magical beings. He'd had the elf wizard imbue a crystal with the spell, and Pembroke had used the crystal to engineer the final product. He called it a "Magic Extractor."

The Extractor was a stick of wood about two feet long, and at the very tip was the spelled crystal with copper wire wrapped around it. The wire continued, wrapped around the length of the stick until it stopped at a terminal above the handle. Also attached to the terminal was more copper wire in a coil. There was a leather strap that kept it coiled and connected to the stick. A battery on the handle connected a trigger switch to the crystal.

The user would point the crystal at a magical item. Pulling the trigger charged the crystal, which would then draw the magical energy from that item. The energy would travel through the copper wire into the ground, where it would disperse. *Genius*, he thought.

He was aware that he was using magic to get away from everyone else's magic, but he didn't care. Self-gratification was all that mattered, everyone else be damned. And now, looking at the items he had created and thinking of all the research he had done on the topic of Earth, he was finally ready to leave. Oriceran could go to any of the hells it chose!

It was illegal to portal to Earth, so he had to be careful. Casting a portal would draw the attention of the authorities, so he journeyed as far away from population centers as he could get. He went to the northernmost part of the Dark Forest. He hadn't done all this work just to be caught making the portal.

He placed his medallion around his neck so non-magicals on Earth would believe he was human. In his right hand, he held the amulet that would create the portal. He began chanting in an ancient language, and the artifact in his hand glowed yellow. Holding it in front of him, he watched as it formed an oval of golden light large enough for him to step through. On the other side of the portal, he saw a green, grassy field, trees nearby, and mountains in the background. There was a clear blue sky overhead. The sight was very beautiful.

He took a deep breath and let out a great sigh. *It's now or never*, he thought. With a great leap, he left the world of Oriceran, hopefully forever, and he entered the world of Earth. What he didn't notice was there were two frightened child ogres who watched him leave. Just before the portal closed, it sucked them through to Earth too.

CHAPTER ONE

Stephanie and Trig ran as fast as they could, which was very fast since both were exceptional athletes and runners. Stephanie often joked that Trig had the stamina of a racehorse.

They were chasing a rat-like creature about the size of a small dog known as a Willen. It was dressed all in black like a little ninja.

Stephanie wanted to laugh at the sight. As members of the Order of the Silver Griffins, Stephanie and Trig had certain spells that allowed them to see other magical creatures whether they were charmed or not. That was why they were able to see the Willen and others couldn't.

The Willen had used magic to commit a theft. Using magic on Earth was a crime in and of itself, and using magic to commit a criminal act was even more serious. As members of the Order of the Silver Griffins, it was Stephanie's and Trig's job to bring the offender to justice, which was why they were now chasing the Willen through the streets of Saint Albans, Vermont.

The chase brought them to an alley where a tall fence partitioned it from the yard of a warehouse. The Willen made it to the fence and found a hole big enough for it to go through but small enough that the witches chasing it couldn't fit. It crawled to the other side.

Stephanie told her partner Trig, "I'll continue following it. See if you can find a way around." With that, she took a running start and climbed the fence to the other side. The Willen had gained ground, so she picked up her pace.

They were outside a warehouse where there were many cargo containers. The Willen whipped around them with ease, but Stephanie felt like she was in a pinball game and she was the ball. At one point she lost sight of it, but then she heard little footsteps on top of a container. She jumped onto the container nearest her and sure enough, a couple of containers over was the Willen.

Stephanie pulled her wand out of a specially installed pocket in her pants and aimed it at the rat-like creature, but before she could cast her spell, she saw sparks bounce off the little ninja. The Willen toppled to the ground with a loud, "OUCH!"

Several warehouse workers heard the Willen's exclamation as it fell and they all turned to look, but thankfully, they didn't see anything.

She looked over to see Trig blowing on the tip of his wand like he was a gunslinger in an old Western.

Stephanie laughed at the sight. "Nice shot, pardner."

He quipped, "Yehaw."

They quickly put restraints on the Willen.

Trig pulled it up onto its feet. "Let's go to the station and process you, little guy."

CHAPTER TWO

Everyone cheered when they arrived at the station. Those Order members who were present all high-fived Stephanie and Trig.

Henry, a weaselly-looking wizard, shouted, "Three arrests in one week! You are like the dynamic duo or something."

Trig grinned at that. "Thanks, Hank. Just doing our job."

Smiddy, another member of the Silver Griffins, added, "Who'd have thought there was so much going on up here in the middle of nowhere? I mean really, Northern Vermont? There's nothing here."

"There's a lot of quartz around here, Smiddy." Stephanie reminded him. "You know how magical beings like quartz. Besides, because there are so few humans here, it's easier for magical Oricerans to hide. That's why we have a branch up here."

Smiddy capitulated. "Yeah, I suppose you're right. Still, three in one week? You two are my new heroes."

Stephanie shook her head but smirked. "We're hardly heroes, but I won't argue."

Stephanie told Trig, "Now for the fun part—all the reports."

"Ugh, I know. The downside to our job," Trig replied. "Hey,

when we're done with all this, you want to go to dinner to celebrate our successful week?"

"Sounds good," Stephanie answered. "Seafood at Jeff's?"

"Seafood at Jeff's," Trig agreed.

Stephanie and Trig had always had a really good working relationship. They had been partners in the Order of the Silver Griffins for a couple of decades. During that time, they had become the very best of friends. Their co-workers had bets as to whether they would become more than just friends, but after the first decade of the two staying friends, the betting pool dwindled and those who had bet on them not becoming a couple won. Only two people won that bet—Stephanie and Trig.

If Stephanie were honest, she would admit that she wouldn't mind being more than friends with Trig. He was very good looking. He had muscles to die for, and a broad chest that she loved. Every now and then brown curls from his hair would fall into his face, and she had to fight the urge to move them out of the way of his striking green eyes.

She believed that Trig had similar feelings for her, but both were afraid to pursue a relationship for fear that it would ruin their friendship.

They were both witches by birth and had been sent to Earth from Oriceran a couple of decades earlier to help keep magic hidden from humans. Each was sent to the Vermont office shortly after graduating training and they hit it off, so they became partners.

She looked at her partner and thought back on the days when they'd first met. She loved her job and being partnered with Trig made it that much better.

He looked up and smiled at her. *Damn*, she thought as she realized she was staring at him. *What the hell is wrong with me?*

Her captain's shout broke through her thoughts. "Steph! Trig! My office!"

She mouthed to Trig, "What did we do now?" Trig just shrugged.

As they entered his office, Captain Bartholomew Rothseth asked them to close the door. They took the two chairs across the desk from where he was sitting.

The imposing wizard just looked at them for a few seconds. The captain often stared to unnerve subordinates. He reminded himself that he didn't want to scare them, so he spoke, "I have another case for you."

Trig said, "But sir, we are just coming off one."

He told them, "I know, and I'm sorry, but we have reports that a portal opened not far from here. It's in the mountains to the east. The portal has since closed, but a farmer from a nearby dairy farm said he saw two odd creatures on his property. They scared his cattle, so he called the police to check them out. Our contact with the state police asked me if we could look into this for them."

The captain continued, "The farmer tried to take a picture, but whatever they were, they were gone by the time he got his phone out."

Trig asked, "Do you have the coordinates of where we believe the portal was?"

"Yes. I'll have the information uploaded to your tablets, as well as any other pertinent information we have at this time."

"Thank you, sir," Trig responded. "How about our contact? We'll need to use police credentials to speak with the farmer. Will he cover for us?"

"Yes, he'll have your back," Captain Rothseth answered.

"OK, then. Once we have the information uploaded, we can head out," Stephanie said after the captain dismissed her and Trig.

As they left their boss's office, Stephanie turned to Trig. "Raincheck on Jeff's?"

Trig nodded. "You bet."

CHAPTER THREE

They pulled up to an old farmhouse in Cabot, Vermont. The front porch was sagging, and there was chipped paint on every inch of the exterior. A rickety door opened and an old man in torn coveralls, mud boots, and a once-white tank top stepped out onto the porch. It creaked with each step he took.

"You the cops? I was told t'expect ya," the old man said.

Trig stepped up. "Yes, sir. And you are Mr. Benoit?"

The farmer nodded. "Yep."

Trig and Stephanie pulled out wallets displaying Vermont State Police badges and IDs. They carried these for just this reason.

"What d'ya need from me?" the farmer asked.

"Well, sir," Stephanie replied, "if you would show us where you saw the odd creatures you reported, we will hopefully find out who or what they are and deal with them as needed."

"Hmph!" the old man exclaimed. He looked carefully at both of them and nodded. "All right, come with me, then."

The farmer brought them by an old barn with about twenty cows filling all the stalls. The ground was muddy, but not so bad that they needed boots.

Stephanie accidentally tripped on a rock. Feeling foolish, her face turned red. Both men thought it was hilarious.

The farmer laughed as he said, "I like you two. Come on, then. We're almost there."

The farmer's property was huge. They followed him to a stand of trees at the end of one of his cow pastures.

He told Stephanie and Trig, "The cows were fussing out here. I came to see what was going on and I saw two...I don't know what they was. They was short. About this tall." He held his hand about the height of his solar plexus. "They had greenish-brown skin and messy hair. They looked like funny-looking kids."

He shook his head at that. "They were big, but they still looked like kids. They didn't look right."

Stephanie told Farmer Benoit, "OK, sir. We'll take a look around and see what we can find."

Trig asked, "Does anything seem out of sorts to you?"

He shook his head. "No. Nothing unusual. Just the creatures and my upset cows."

They came to the trees where Farmer Benoit said he had seen the strange beings. "They was right over there." He pointed to a spot in the woods.

Trig thanked Mr. Benoit. "Unless you want to stay, we will take it from here. It's your property, and we don't want to over-step our welcome."

Mr. Benoit said, "It's no problem. If you don't need me, I'll be heading back. Thank you for coming out so quickly."

He began walking away, then stopped. As an afterthought, he turned and asked, "If you find anything out, can you please let me know one way or the other? You have my number?"

"Yes, sir," said Stephanie. "We'll call you once we know something either way."

"Thank you," he said and left.

Once he was out of range, Trig and Stephanie turned to each other.

"What are you thinking?" asked Trig.

"From the files we received and from what Mr. Benoit said, it sounds like ogres, but they are too short, from the descriptions we have been given."

Trig looked thoughtful. "Hmm. Children, maybe?"

Stephanie nodded. "That's a good working hypothesis. Let's see if there is anything around here."

As Trig was looking for clues or evidence, he said, "You know, if they are alone, they could still be nearby. They might not have wandered."

Stephanie agreed. "There haven't been any more sightings. If there were, the captain would have called."

Trig looked at his phone. "He may have. No signal."

Stephanie smiled at him. "Both a benefit, and a hindrance of working up here. Benefit if you don't want the captain to get hold of you. Hindrance if you need the captain to get hold of you."

Trig laughed at her. "You want your cake, and you want to eat it too."

Stephanie gave a big smile. "Yep! You know it."

She looked around the area. "The plants and trees around here have a lot of damage." She made a sweeping motion with her hand. "Whoever it was didn't seem to make any effort to remain hidden."

Trig knelt, checking an area that appeared extremely disturbed. "There was a lot of movement around here. There are a lot of boot prints, and they are wide compared to their length, similar to an ogre's. We probably are looking at young ogres."

He looked closer at the footprints. "Look here, Steph. There's another type of print here. It looks different than these other two sets." He looked up at her. "There are three sets of prints."

Stephanie looked at the prints with Trig. "Mr. Benoit said that he only saw the two ogre kids. I wonder where the other individual went?"

They both stood, and Trig looked down the path left by what

they believed to be ogre children. "It looks like these two tracks go off in a different direction than this other set. We should probably find the kids first."

Stephanie added, "If that is what they are."

Trig shrugged and smiled. "Working hypothesis."

CHAPTER FOUR

They followed a trail of torn tree limbs, smashed plants, and crushed underbrush until they came to a nearby farm, where a man was aiming a shotgun at two individuals cowering on the ground. Sure enough, they were ogre children.

Stephanie ran forward, yelling, "STOP! Don't shoot!" while Trig quickly aimed his wand at the person holding the gun. Magic flew from its tip and struck the human in his center mass. The human, a short, stocky man, dropped to the ground, unconscious.

Stephanie looked at the kids. "It's OK. I'm a witch." She pointed at Trig. "He's a wizard. We're both with the Order of the Silver Griffins. Let's get away from here so the farmer won't see you."

Trig said, "We need to hurry. He's only sleeping and will wake soon. Take the children to the car, and I'll remove this man's memory of any of this."

Stephanie nodded and walked with both ogres back to their vehicle, which was still at the entrance to Farmer Benoit's driveway.

Trig watched them leave, then put his hands on the sides of

the farmer's head and spoke ancient words. When he was satisfied that he had removed any memory of the ogre children, he woke the farmer up.

Trig helped the man to his feet. "Sir, are you OK? You were out cold."

The farmer stood up on wobbly legs. "I… I don't know. What happened? I was coming outside." He paused as he looked around confused. "The dogs were barking. I came out to see what was happening and, I don't remember." He looked at Trig. "Who are you?"

"Ah, I'm sorry. My name is Trig Lothren. I'm with the State Police." He showed the farmer his fake badge. "We were investigating your neighbor's property. He said he saw some trespassers on his land and they were upsetting his cows."

The farmer shook his head. "I don't know anything about that. Nothing unusual has happened here. That is, until the dogs started barking."

Sure enough, a couple of mutts were standing on the front porch of the old farmhouse, sniffing and looking in the direction of the woods. "They must have heard me walking up the path. They were most likely barking at me."

"Yeah, that must be it." The farmer shook his head, still confused.

Trig handed the man his card. "If you see anything unusual, would you please let me know? I'm at this number."

They shook hands, and the farmer said, "Sure. I'll call if I hear of anything."

"Thank you." Trig waved goodbye as he walked down the farmer's driveway.

Stephanie and the two ogres were waiting by their sedan.

"How'd it go?" she asked Trig.

MICHAEL ANDERLE

He shrugged. "He'll call if anything comes up."

"What'd he just do to the farmer?" the ogre boy asked Stephanie.

"He made certain that the farmer won't remember seeing you. We can't have humans knowing about magic and magical beings, at least not yet." She looked at both children. "Are you two OK? Are you hurt?"

"No. We aren't hurt," the boy ogre said. He looked down at his body and then at his sister's. "I think we're OK."

"He was gonna kill us?" the girl asked.

"No, hon. I think he was just scared, and he wanted to frighten you away." She smiled at them. "What are your names?"

The boy said, "My name is Roderick. This is my sister Petunia."

"Nice to meet you, Roderick and Petunia. My name is Stephanie. My friends will sometimes call me Steph. And the wizard over there," she pointed toward Trig, "is my partner Trig."

Petunia spoke up. "You said you were from the Silver Griffins. We've heard of you. You put people in jail for using magic on Earth. You won't put us in jail, will you? We didn't make the magic that brought us here. That mean gnome did."

That piqued Stephanie's interest. "You didn't make the portal?"

Roderick answered, "No, ma'am. Like my sister said, it was a gnome."

"Do you know who this gnome is?"

Petunia said, "No, ma'am. We never saw him before. He was walking through the forest near our home, and he was throwing and breaking things. He scared us, so we hid. He came up really close to us when he cast the portal spell, and it felt like it was pulling us. Before we knew what was happening, it sucked us in, and we ended up here. Is this Earth?"

Stephanie nodded.

Roderick continued the story. "When we landed on this side,

we saw the gnome hurrying away. We didn't know how to get back, but we didn't want to go near the gnome because he scared us, so we went the other direction looking for help. That's when the farmer came out and was gonna shoot us."

Stephanie nodded in understanding. "It's OK. We'll get you back to Oriceran. In the meantime, my partner Trig, and I have to find this gnome. You said he went that way?" she asked, pointing in the direction they had suggested.

Roderick said, "Yes, ma'am."

They all climbed into the sedan. The two children sat in the back, Stephanie sat in the passenger seat, and Trig drove. On the drive to the next farmhouse, Stephanie phoned the captain to update him on the situation.

When they came to the next farmhouse, Trig parked the vehicle at the end of the drive. Stephanie turned around and asked the kids to stay in the vehicle while she and Trig spoke to the residents.

Petunia pleaded with both adults. "Please don't leave us here alone. Let us come with you."

Roderick said, "We'll be good. Honest."

Stephanie smiled at both of them. They were very polite children, especially for ogres. "Kids, I'm not worried about you causing trouble. It's just that humans aren't used to seeing ogres. You are magical beings, and they don't have much magic here. Also, we don't know anything about this gnome. If he's mean like you think he is, he might be dangerous."

Roderick looked at her with big, sad eyes. "But doesn't that mean that we shouldn't be left alone?"

Stephanie sighed and then smiled. "Yes. Yes, it does. OK, you can come, but you need to remain out of the humans' sight, OK?"

Roderick and Petunia nodded.

Trig smiled at Stephanie. "You'd make a good mom."

She smacked his arm.

He turned to the kids. "Are we all set, then?"

Everyone nodded, so he said. "OK, let's go. Kids, stay hidden behind us." They heard a couple of OKs.

From the barn came the sounds of animals in distress. The cows sounded like they were in pain. With a look of concern, Trig turned to Stephanie and said, "I know that sound. When dairy cows miss a milking, it becomes painful."

Stephanie's eyebrows lifted.

He put both hands up and said, "I'm not a dairy farmer, but I've lived around them most of my life. One of my neighbors had a farm that lost power, and it took them a couple of hours to get their generator running. The cows were in a lot of pain until they could start milking again." He looked sad. "They were considering putting some of them out of their misery if they couldn't get power back on to the milking machines." Trig shook his head at the memory. "I don't think I could do the job of a farmer."

Looking in the direction of the distressed cows, he said, "I'll go look at the barn. Do you want to go check the farmhouse?"

Stephanie nodded. "Sure. Be careful."

Trig grinned at her. "Back at ya, partner."

Stephanie smiled as she walked up the driveway toward the house. When she got closer, she motioned for the children to hide, and they slid behind the trees along the side of the drive.

CHAPTER FIVE

Knowing the children were well hidden, she continued to walk up the driveway to the house. She didn't want any more humans to have their memories wiped, so she hoped they would remain concealed.

Pembroke was sitting on the porch contemplating his new life on Earth. He took a long drag from his pipe. Looking toward the drive, he saw a woman walking toward him. *Well, hell*, he thought.

He pulled a dagger from his waistband and placed it under the chair cushion in such a way that he could easily grab it if needed. He waited for the lady to walk to him.

Stephanie stopped at the stairs that led to the porch. "Hello, sir," she greeted the man while presenting her badge to him. "I was wondering if you could answer a few questions? It's regarding an issue that occurred earlier today."

She looked closely at him. She could see that he was a gnome. His charm didn't work on witches.

Pembroke didn't want to deal with this, but he thought better of it and played along. "An issue? From this morning? I'll answer what I can, officer, but I have been here all day, so I don't know what kind of help I can give you."

"Fair enough," she said as she reached for the wand in her pocket. "Maybe you can start by telling me what a gnome is doing sitting on a farmhouse's porch only hours after a portal from Oriceran reportedly opened nearby?"

Pembroke didn't even think, he instinctively reached for his hidden dagger and flung it toward the woman in front of him. He was aiming for her center mass, but the dagger missed its target and struck her in the thigh, just missing the femoral artery. It caused her to fall to her knees.

As she was falling, Stephanie was able to get a shot off with her wand. A ball of flame just missed hitting the gnome in his forehead. Instead, the fireball managed to fly past his bald head, singing his ear.

Stephanie crawled behind a tree for cover. Propping her back against the tree, she pulled the dagger out of her leg. Pressing down on her wound with one hand and holding tightly to her wand with the other, she turned to take another shot at the gnome but heard the door open and close. The gnome was no longer on the porch.

Grimacing, she stood and loudly said, "Kids, get Trig, but stay away from the house. I don't want either of you getting hurt."

She saw Petunia run toward the barn. Roderick must have stayed put. This gnome was dangerous. She hoped the children remained hidden.

Not seeing anyone looking out from the house, she felt it was safe, so she limped toward the door. Her leg throbbed and it was very difficult for her to stay focused.

Pulling herself up the porch stairs, she made it to the front door. She stayed off to the side for cover as she tried to open it, but the gnome must have managed to lock the door when he went inside.

Stephanie said a short incantation as she pointed her wand at the lock. There was a click as her magic unlocked the door.

Still using the side of the door for cover, she carefully pushed the door open.

Immediately her senses were overwhelmed by the sickly scent of death. It was so intense that she wanted to vomit. She momentarily closed her eyes, not wanting to think about what she might see when she went into the house.

The hallway was clear of any immediate danger, so she slowly made her way inside. Sure enough, on the floor were the bodies of an elderly man and woman. A sense of grief fell over her, but she quickly squelched it. She'd grieve later. She had to focus on subduing the psychotic gnome.

Pembroke was hiding behind a display cabinet in the dining room. He had a wand out and pointing at the room's entrance. As she limped past, he was able to take a quick shot at her.

His fireball struck Stephanie in her abdomen, and she doubled over from the force of the blast and the pain of the burns. She successfully patted out the flames on her shirt, but the fireball had managed to penetrate her abdomen. Blood oozed from the wound, and she could smell her burnt skin.

The loss of blood, first from her thigh and now from her abdomen, was starting to make her woozy and she was afraid she would lose consciousness. With her back against the wall, she slid down to the floor.

Damn, she thought. This psychopathic gnome has some skill, or he's the luckiest son of a bitch who ever lived. Or I'm the stupidest agent who ever lived for coming in here without a backup or any healing potions.

Out loud she said, "If I'm going to die here, I'm going out on my terms." She turned to face the dining room. When she saw the tip of a wand come up, she quickly aimed her wand at it and let loose with a fireball.

The fireball hit Pembroke's arm, causing him to drop his wand. Stephanie shot another fireball in his direction that hit the gnome in the shoulder before she passed out from blood loss and pain.

Pembroke was also in pain, but he wasn't out of the fight yet. Seeing that the woman was down but not dead, he went into the hallway where he had left his bag. He pulled out the Magic Extractor he'd brought with him from Oriceran.

He unhooked the coil of copper wire and looked around for a place to ground the staff's magic. The floor of the farmhouse wouldn't work since it was wood, but there was a potted plant nearby. It wasn't large, but with luck, the amount of dirt it held would hold the magical energy from the device's crystal. He put the tip of the copper coil in the plant's dirt, aimed the crystal point toward the unconscious agent, and pulled the trigger. The crystal started glowing.

As expected, the crystal pulled the magic from Stephanie and sent it into the potted plant's soil. Pembroke was elated. His invention worked! *How exciting*, he thought.

Before the strange contraption had finished draining her, though, Trig burst into the house.

Pembroke dropped the Extractor and ran farther inside and went down the stairs to the basement. Trig was going to follow him, but he saw Stephanie unconscious on the floor.

Trig knew that she was injured, but there was nothing he could do at that moment. When he lifted her head and tried waking her, Steph's eyes opened and she weakly told him, "Go…get…him. He…needs…to be…stopped." Her eyes closed again, but she was still conscious.

He shook his head, but he knew she was right. With tears in his eyes, he told her, "I'll be back. You better still be alive."

She gave him a weak smile and opened her eyes again to look at him. "Go!"

As Trig was chasing the gnome into the basement, the two ogre children snuck into the house. Seeing Stephanie on the floor, Petunia ran to her. In her hand was a little vial containing an orange liquid. She poured the liquid down Stephanie's throat and sent a prayer to her goddess.

Stephanie opened her eyes and looked at the young ogre. She weakly thanked the girl.

It didn't take long for Stephanie to start feeling better. She could feel her health returning, but she still felt like something was missing.

She forced herself to sit up, which was hard because she was still very weak. Rubbing her head, she asked, "What happened?"

Petunia answered, "You were hurt pretty bad. That gnome tried to kill you, but Trig chased him away." She held up the vial so Stephanie could see it. "I gave you some of our healing potion, although it's made for ogres, so I wasn't sure if it would work. Mom makes us carry some when we go out into the Dark Forest. It wasn't enough to heal you completely. I'm sorry."

Stephanie shook her head. "No need to be sorry, honey. You did well. You saved my life today. For that, I will be forever indebted to you."

Stephanie looked around the room. There was blood everywhere, some dry from the dead farmers and some still sticky from her. She saw a strange contraption lying on the floor, a stick with wire wrapped around it and a crystal attached to it. The end of the wire had been stuck into the dirt of a potted plant. At first, she was confused, and then she knew why she felt like a part of her was missing.

Holding up her wand, she tried to cast a fireball at the plant, but nothing happened. She pointed the wand at a vase on the table and tried casting a fireball at it. Once again, nothing happened. Her magic was gone. Panic set in; she was scared. As a witch, magic was her essence, her very being, and now she had none.

She heard noises coming from the basement. *Trig!* He was in danger and she had no magic, but somehow, she had to help him. She had to save Trig, so she pushed herself up off the floor.

Turning to the children, she said, "Stay here, kids. I have to take care of the gnome once and for all. You two are special, and I need you to stay safe. OK?" She had only known them for a couple of hours, but she was becoming very fond of them.

They nodded, and Stephanie limped as fast as she could to the basement. At the entrance, a cane was lying against a wall. With no other weapon available, she grabbed it.

She could hear a scuffle. It sounded like there was a really good fight happening. When she got to the bottom step, she saw Trig and Pembroke throwing punches at each other.

The shorter gnome ran into Trig's midsection and slammed him into shelves holding canning materials. Glass jars went flying everywhere, and the fighters fell into the pile of broken glass and wooden boards.

Pembroke placed his good hand over Trig's face, trying to crush his head into the debris. Trig's right hand was free, and he managed to punch the gnome in the arm that had been injured by Stephanie's fireball.

Pembroke screamed and lost his balance for a moment, which was enough of a distraction for Trig to push the gnome off him. Once Trig regained his balance, he gave the gnome a kick in the gut.

The gnome was hit so hard that he flew toward Stephanie, where she was holding the cane like a baseball bat as she balanced on one leg. When the gnome came near her, she swung as hard as she could, striking his back right below the neck. He flew across the room, unconscious as he hit the wall.

Trig smiled broadly as he yelled, "It's a HOME RUN!"

He handed her his wand so she could send the psychotic gnome to the Silver Griffin lockup. "Do you want to do the honors?"

She sighed heavily and sat down on the bottom step. "I'd love to, but unfortunately, this piece of shit stole my magic."

Trig laughed. "Yeah. OK." He shook his head. "No, really, do you want the honors of sending him to lockup?"

Stephanie's face didn't change. She still looked beaten. "No, really, he stole my magic. My poof was pilfered."

Trig didn't know how to react. He had never heard of that happening before. He pointed the wand at Pembroke, said an incantation, and the gnome disappeared, magically transported to the Order of the Silver Griffins' headquarters.

Trig turned back to Stephanie. "*He stole your magic*? Really? How did that happen?"

She explained about the magic-extracting device Pembroke had used.

Trig responded, "That thing is dangerous. Where is it now? It should be locked away. Better yet, it should be destroyed.

As Stephanie got to her feet, Trig pulled her to him and hugged her. Kissing the top of her head, he said, "We'll fix this. We'll make it right. Come on, let's go back to the office. We'll take care of the kids and get you looked at."

Stephanie nodded, thinking that even without her magic, she was enjoying this moment.

They stopped in the hall on their way out of the house. The kids were still there and Stephanie hugged them both, glad they were OK. She let them know that the gnome was in custody and no longer a threat.

Trig called for the cleaners. There were still two dead bodies, and evidence all over the place that showed Trig and Stephanie had been here.

While Trig was making the call, Stephanie went to the Magic Extractor, which was lying on the floor next to the pot. The wire still in the dirt, and she thought she saw the plant glow. "That can't be right," she said out loud.

Trig was watching her as he was talking on the phone.

It looked to Stephanie like her magical energy was stuck in the cramped space of the planter with nowhere to go. She touched the glowing plant, and immediately felt a rush of energy as magic—her magic—flowed back into her. She sucked in a huge breath at the power that suddenly raged through her, and stumbled backward.

"Holy shit!" she exclaimed. "It's back!" She turned to look at Trig and said again, "It's back!" She let out a huge laugh. The rush of magic had healed the last of her wounds, and she felt great.

She left the magic extractor where it was. When the cleaners arrived, they would take care of it, as well as the bodies and blood. There would be nothing left on the property to show that they had ever been there.

She sighed. There was still a lot of work to do back at the office. They had reports to write, and two wonderful ogre children needed to get back to their family.

EPILOGUE

Thankfully the rest of their day was uneventful.

Once they got approval, they took Roderick and Petunia through a portal to Oriceran. Their mother was waiting for them as the portal opened. She was a very big ogre, but also a very happy one. The Order had been able to get word to Oriceran and had let the ogre parents know that the two children were OK. They were very grateful. Stephanie hugged the two children before stepping into the portal to return home.

Before they started writing their reports, both the captain and Trig insisted that Stephanie get checked out by the Order's medic, and thankfully she received a clean bill of health. Somehow, she had completely healed when her magic returned to her. Her magic wasn't the healing kind, so that surprised her, but she wasn't going to question it since she felt great.

It was starting to get late when they finished the last of the reports. Trig stood up and put out a hand for Stephanie to take. "It may be too late for Jeff's. Raincheck?"

Stephanie smiled and nodded. "Raincheck."

"Nellie's is still open. Do you want to go dancing?" As an

afterthought, he looked at her and said, "By the way, I will consider this a date."

She smiled at him. "Hell, yes! It's a date. Let's go dancing."

He gave her a big smile in return and offered her his arm.

They walked by the captain as they were leaving and they heard him mutter, "It's about damn time!" as they left the building.

FINIS

AUTHOR'S NOTES

Honestly, I have no idea how I came up with the idea of Pembroke. I just started thinking about a gnome who was upset with his life working in the library and ran with it. I didn't start out imagining him being so angry, but that's how he ended up after writing him.

I was a police officer when I was younger and in shape. I tried to write Stephanie and Trig the way I remember. Hopefully, everyone enjoys these two.

Story-writing is enjoyable for me. I hope my enjoyment transfers to the written page. I will write stories regardless, but if other people gain enjoyment from them, I am even happier.

Thank you for reading *All in a Day's Work*. I hope you enjoyed reading it as much as I did writing it.

— Lisa

SOUTHWEST STYLE

BY CRAIG LEWIS

Poverty and lack of opportunity can lead to a vicious cycle. Lack of local opportunity compels anyone seeking better to seek it elsewhere. This is particularly true when such individuals were in fact exceptional enough to be noticed even among bigger fish in a big pool. Those who choose to remain with their roots and protect and guide those who would otherwise be forgotten can well be considered heroes.

Dedicated to Martha Carr and Michael Anderle for building a sandbox then inviting us in to play, and to all the authors whose works fire the dreams to let us travel outside ourselves.

PRELUDE

School of Necessary Magic, Three Years Ago

The room had extensive reinforcement, both magical and mundane. It was one of several on the campus of the School of Necessary Magic, but this was one of the strongest. Past experience with the experiment about to be conducted suggested this was absolutely necessary.

The room contained few items. A long, spare steel table contained a vacuum-sealed bag exceptionally heavy for its size, and a tiny open dish of empowered liquid silver. And a ferret, sitting on the edge with its eyes closed in an attitude that clearly demonstrated complete attention to its surroundings.

Other than the ferret, two young males stood across from each other near the middle of the table. Discerning people would see flashes of the shielding spells maintained by the faculty members monitoring the experiment from the room's observation area.

The Light Elf's hands were poised. "We've got everything down. I can feel it. Ready when you are." The human nodded. He'd call the cadence until the process was complete...or the experiment blew up. Again.

"Join and form the mold." Two lines of power emerged from the mages, passing to—no, *through*—the ferret. The converged line was denser and more powerful than either source line.

The human shaped the emergent line. First came a long, mostly flat and narrow shape, obscured slightly by the power's radiance. Next came a pair of bands circumscribing the central shape, one horizontally oriented, the other vertically. All participants, and clearly this included the ferret, paused to inspect the new construct briefly.

"Injection." The sealed packet rose, to be sliced open with a gesture. The contents, an advanced powdered steel, were directed into the mold.

"Refine." Students of sword forms could now recognize the shape, or at least its influence, as Japanese: roughly a *wakizashi* with an integrated guard. Even the groove was present. A purist might object; the *tsuka* was far too short.

"Set." The ferret nodded as it took control of the field for now, freeing the mages to power the next stages.

"Pulse." This was the first stage where destructive failure might occur, but it had been some time since that had happened. An electromagnetic pulse of high intensity but exceptional brevity converted the powdered steel into something with a much more structured appearance.

"Heat." This took time. The mages poured energy into the metal steadily until a dull red glow emerged. The vertical and horizontal bands trapped and recirculated the thermal energy radiating from the form.

"Scribe." The human held the heat stable while the elf adjusted the pressure field. Various runes were being traced into the *shinogi*, the blade ridge above the groove, which was a delicate process. The runes had to be drawn precisely, and the entire rune construct was connected. Editing didn't work; they'd learned that, too. No, a mistake would force the entire scribing phase to start over.

Some minutes later, the elf paused to catch his breath. Both heavily sweating mages reviewed the completed runes with approval.

"Silver." This was the companion phase. The runes did nothing without the silver. It flowed into the etched lines as the field was reshaped to lay out the runes onto the metal, leaving glittering tracework flush with the still-dark steel. As Sedrec completed the silver injection, Ramon clamped the field even tighter to lock it into the rune pattern.

"Vise." The mages took control of the form again, increasing the pressure to about five hundred psi. This was far from enough to execute the sintering, but it greatly aided the overall stability to do this. This fact had been identified by the elf during early process reviews.

"Build charges." The elf had control of the pressure field. His job would be to crush the metal with twenty thousand psi at the right time. The human prepared a small, intense, carefully calibrated lightning strike. The combination would complete the electro-sintering process...or explode spectacularly.

"Sinter charge ready."

"Pressure pulse ready." The elf insisted on having a line in the script...and it was his responsibility anyway. They couldn't hold this kind of power for long, either.

"OK, Felicia, on my count." The ferret, actually a spirit who preferred to manifest in its current form, would trigger the spells. The sinter took only thousandths of a second, and mortal reaction times were inadequate to ensure simultaneity. And if it went bad...

"Three...two...one...*now*!"

The flash was dazzling.

The form...

HELD!

The mostly finished sword blade floated serenely. The work wasn't done, not yet; they still had to anneal, then quench the blade while empowering and then sealing the runes. These steps were equally important, but low-risk. The mages performed them with due diligence considering the massive effort to reach this point, and the fatigue, physical and magical, it had caused. After another half-hour's work, the blade was complete. Blue energy rippled through the runes as a minor light spell was boosted to flashbulb intensity.

They'd done it. Ramon Montero and Sedrec the Light Elf had successfully completed their joint senior project—and Ramon had his sword's blade.

Sedrec would have to wait a few weeks for his.

CHAPTER ONE

Las Cruces, New Mexico

The morning Mass in Spanish had concluded some time ago, but five people had remained after inside the small Holy Family church. One was an older gentleman dressed soberly, albeit lacking a clerical collar. He was inspecting and lightly polishing the ciborium, by which task his position became evident: sacristan. Two others were teenage boys, dressed casually but in spotlessly clean clothing as they restored the nave area, refreshed the consumed votives, and generally helped set the church back to rights.

The last two—one human, one Light Elf—had just finished swapping an old pew in need of restoration for one that had recently received that attention when from each of their pockets the same curious sound emerged.

"Privateering, we will go
Privateering, Yoh! oh! ho!
Privateering, we will go
Yeah! oh! oh! ho!"

Ramon Montero answered before the Knopfler lines started

again, giving the sacristan a sheepish glance. That ringtone, one of three, suggested that taking this call was not optional.

"Spellswords, this is Ramon." Spellswords was the business he and his partner, the elf across the pew, ran—part bounty hunting, part Anti-Enhanced Threat support team. Las Cruces, New Mexico wasn't exactly up to paying for full-time AET support, so at need, the pair provided their services at rates the local governments could handle.

"Mr. Montero, I'm glad I reached you. My name is Jim Thomas and I oversee the White Sands Reserve." The Reserve primarily entailed the land that had formerly been the White Sands Missile Range south of US 70. The range had been decommissioned as a military base a decade before. Given a stark lack of motivation to attempt commercial development, the area had been turned into a desert wildlife preserve. "We have an incident with some...non-native wildlife, and we would like your company's assistance. It's nothing any of us have heard of, including a Wood Elf the Gardener sent."

Montero glanced at his elven partner Sedrec, who had been listening on his phone and now gave him a thumbs-up.

"One moment, please." He covered his phone and addressed the sacristan. "Sorry, we're gonna have to bug. They're having problems in Mordor."

The man turned to the boys. "Finish that up and you're done for today. Two more weeks, though! And if you give Mr. Santos any problems? Don't. Right?" The boys averred they'd be good. Ramon turned his attention back to his caller as he and Sedrec started out to their car.

"Sorry; just wrapping up something. OK, so what's the word?"

"We're doing population studies, as you know, mostly using drones. Audio picked up an unusual high-pitched sound—something like a roar in falsetto, they said. The camera caught a brief glimpse of a critter that looked to have two heads. One was dog-like, the other reptilian, best they could tell...because right then darts or something flew up and blew the drone away."

"Belial's bleeding balls! Fine, the darts make it sound like a manticore, but two heads? Some dickwad on the Oriceran side probably dumped the results of a magic experiment here so he doesn't get blamed for it."

"Yes, and I'll file a report at the Palace if so. That's illegal experimentation even in Oriceran. Mr. Thomas, this is Sedrec. Where and when are you staging? We're gearing up now."

"White Sands HQ, and ASAP."

"I know the missile park adequately, so we'll be there in less than five minutes."

"What?" Mr. Thomas' reactions were still not conditioned to a magical world, but his position required a somewhat greater knowledge of it than many. Portals were handy. "It's a twenty minute drive... Oh. Right. Great! See you there shortly, then."

As the pair completed their preparations, using gear from the magically secured case in the trunk—what looked to be light ballistic vests, desert hiking boots, Glock 41s with extra clips, light packs, and of course their personal runeswords from which they took the company name—the other "partner" darted across the grass from the garden and jumped onto the hood, and then to the roof.

Ramon looked at the ferret now peering at him. "You get lucky? Hope so, cuz we don't have time to hit the house for a snack." The ferret sent him images of yippy little dogs that must have belonged to neighbors with a general sense of disgust.

Ramon just laughed. "Well we're heading to Mordor, so who knows? You might get a bite over there." He held out his arm for Felicia, his pet/friend/familiar/guardian spirit, so she could ride in her usual place on his right shoulder. Felicia didn't have a problem with churches, but they weren't her favorite places.

Sedrec just smiled. "I presume you and Her Majesty are now ready?" He was already opening the portal.

CHAPTER TWO

White Sands Main Post

Four humans, a female Light Elf, and a male Wood Elf were at the park when they stepped through the portal. Sedrec darted over to give the Light Elf a bear hug, and the oldest human came to shake hands with Ramon.

"Mr. Montero, I'm Jim Thomas. Glad you got here so fast. Not sure how long this'll take, and I do *not* want to give this thing any more of a chance to make trouble than I have to." He started the introductions as the others (sans the hugging, chattering Light Elves) came forward. "This here is Dan Mirles. He's one of our licensed wardens." The weather-beaten man nodded, his rifle in cradle carry. "This is Eric Armstrong. Ex-Army; used to be stationed here, in fact. He knows the ground." Armstrong preferred a sling carry, and he'd clearly taken his gear with him after discharge. "And this is Stan Davidson. He's our comms guy. Drones are being run from HQ, and they talk to him."

The Light Elves sauntered up as the Wood Elf spoke. "I am Marben. Given the nature of this preserve, the Gardener felt supervision was prudent, and he chose me for that role. I've seen salamanders, firehawks, minor basilisks, and even a few lesser drakes. All ordinary enough, for Oriceran anyway, and no real threat. But this? I have *no* idea."

"So that probably means it's illegal, so he fetched me." The female Light Elf smiled at the group, then focused on Ramon. "I'm Treasa...and yes, I'm Sed's distant cousin. We haven't seen much of each other in years! You must be his boyfriend?"

"And here you had me worried I was finding one of his old flames. Yep, I'm Ramon. Nice to meet you." He gave her a hug; he had technically been family since his and Sedrec's joining ceremony.

"Nice to meet all of you. Tall, blond, and dour is my partner Sedrec, and on my shoulder is Felicia. She should be a big help finding this thing and probably keeping everyone from becoming a pincushion if this is anything like a manticore.

"We're both registered class-five bounty hunters and fully licensed mages. We're also about the closest there is to an AET-level response in the area, and we have state authorization. El Paso has a swarm of bounty hunters, but they're...not civic-minded. Considering Juarez, they don't need to be, I suppose. Tell us what you can do, so we know what *we* need to do. Dan?"

"Physical enhancements, thanks to a useful artifact. Stronger and tougher than usual, don't care about the heat, and I heal fairly fast."

Eric nodded. "No artifacts but sniper trained. Very accurate ranging and sight to about a thousand yards, not that we're likely to have a shot that long, not out here." The old Missile Range terrain only *looked* flat, and mesquite dotted the landscape as well, offering cover to anything low to the ground. Given the basilisks and salamanders, it wasn't the safest of places.

Treasa and Marden had bows and elven abilities, so Ramon wasn't worried about them. "OK, so do we know where the thing is?"

Eric answered, "It was about six or seven miles east out Nike Avenue, where the various launch sites were—which should cut down on the cross-country. The road's not in great shape, but it's a lot better than hauling ass cross-country."

Ramon was the public face. Sedrec was stronger tactically. "We have to think it heard the drone and took exception to it. We need to nail down its location, and the final approach will have to be on foot. I don't think the tail spikes are too much of a threat, but only if we know where they're coming from. Stan, how many drones do you have that can work this scrub?"

"Just two that can cover any kind of ground. Front view. I'll have both on a split screen."

"Excellent. Felicia, if Your Majesty would be so kind as to follow the road—let's say, out to this complex, LC-35. That's a good outer limit for now, I think. Stan, have the drones fly five hundred meters to either side. If that doesn't work, we'll plan some other passes as time permits."

Ramon looked at Felicia. "And if you eat a basilisk or salamander, you know damn well you're banned from the house for the night...at least. And pace the drones, please. You'll see them; the drone operators won't see you."

The humans' faces were etched with concern: was this guy sane? Having the ferret issue a wheezy, toothy *hic-hic* sound that was blatantly laughter didn't help much. Seeing Felicia change into her spirit form, which was translucent and caused the sunlight to prism everywhere, stunned them into belief.

Felicia flew off as the drones fired up and started on their track.

CHAPTER THREE

White Sands

The first indication was another round of spikes heading for the northern drone, but they missed. Sedrec had told the drone to pull back. Ramon had Felicia fly overwatch as everyone piled into the ATVs. The few miles were covered quickly, but to Ramon's disgust, not quite fast enough.

Felicia didn't have to travel line of sight...and there had been a fat basilisk lounging under a mesquite. Gah! Her ferret form didn't have the usual scent glands, but post-basilisk, she'd smell worse than a wet bear who'd pissed off a herd of skunks.

Soon after that, though, she had "eyes" back on the...thing. Definitely chimeric, totally ugly. Initial reports were accurate enough, but completely inadequate. The left head was canid...if you counted hell hounds as dog-like. Black on black with glowing red eyes. The right head and neck resembled a monitor lizard's. And the wings, spiked back, and tail were pure manti-core. Ramon used the picture passed to him by Felicia to create an image of the beast for Marben to examine. The Wood Elf was not amused.

"Whatever pea-brained pus-ball dreamed that up? Of course,

he lost control! None of those are readily controllable, much less after cramming everything together. I'm amazed it lived. I want to flay his skin off and stake him to a fire ant mound.

"But if he got the combination to be functional, everything probably works, so closing invites the hell hound's fire breath. And figure the lizzy's bite is effectively, if not actually, poison. Hell, figure the spikes are too. Good news is the rifles should hurt it, and our arrows will definitely cause it grief."

Sedrec laid out the tactical plan. "Two groups. Ramon, you've got the humans. Aim for two hundred yards or so southwest. We'll aim for two hundred to the southeast. I'd love to fire together, but that's probably not going to work. Sorry, guys, but we're quieter than you are, and this...chimericore...hears too well, if it heard the drones. I fear it will focus on you, but that shouldn't be a problem. If it opens up on you, take any safe shots you can— especially you, Eric. Head shots are your best bet, but don't be foolish. If it's focused on you, *we* should have easy shots."

Dan was worried. "Not a *problem*? Did you see how fast those spikes flew?"

"Not a problem because Sed and I will have shield spells up. Marben and Treasa have their own defenses...maybe layered shielding? Dunno; they'll work that out. For us, Felicia is a guardian spirit. She augments anything defensive. So, yeah, I'm not too worried."

It went without a hitch. The drones swung around and flew in from the north. Everyone wanted this recorded. Their mild buzz alerted the chimericore, but when it heard the crackle from the approaching humans, it wasn't sure where to focus. First blood went to Eric, but his shot only drilled the reptilian neck. The canid head stared balefully as the creature discharged a massive volley of spines...much too slowly. The shield was firmly in place, and the spines—six inches of hard, bone-like material as pointed as any crossbow quarrel—simply exploded into powder.

"And...*now!*" Ramon turned the shield into a web, and both rifles let loose with bursts. The canid head lost an eye. The other rounds inflicted painful but minor wounds. Again, the creature's response was both slow and telegraphed. Another volley of spines arrived, this time accompanied by an ugly black and green wad of...something spit by the lizard's head. Ramon channeled through his sword to harden and expand the shield. Getting splashed by that stuff couldn't be healthy.

The sizzling sounds from the plants that *did* get splashed confirmed that.

From the east, Oriceran arrows slammed into the creature's body, inflicting further pain and confusion.

"One more time...three, two, one, *now!*" Ramon called for another burst. This cost the canid head part of its jaw...and its temper. Manticore seemed to be the dominant component, and manticores were aggressive. It took to the air, but that could best be described as a blunder. Manticores are terrible fliers, and now it had no cover whatsoever. Arrows and a small fireball smashed into it, wreaking further havoc. Its effort to return fire was wild as it thrashed.

Then everyone opened up. Sedrec dropped his shield to secondary and Felicia took over maintenance on Ramon's. The arrows and bullets slammed home first, and a pair of white-hot fire bolts admirably completed the job.

When the smoking, stinking carcass hit the ground, a great cheer, like the home crowd celebrating a walk-off home run, erupted. Sedrec groaned inwardly; Felicia was developing a sense of humor much too close to Ramon's.

CHAPTER FOUR

Las Cruces

The portal opened up at the church where they'd left the car. To offload the combat gear into the trunk, Sedrec took the keys as Ramon stared down his ferret.

"Told you not to. No, you *don't* get a ride back to the house, Felicia. You're exiled to the backyard tonight!" Even Sedrec could sense her mood...totally worth it. Not like Ramon was angry, not really, but still...

"Come on, let's grab a shower. We'll hit up Zeffiro, then take the night off."

"Hmm. Are you trying to use wood-fired pizza to take advantage of me?"

"Damn straight."

Ramon groaned. "*That* line means you owe me a back rub as well!"

"That was going to be the opening act, yes."

They were driving up to their house now. "Oh...well, then. Hey, is that Clouseau barking?"

"No other dog in the area is a bass, but it sounds playful."

"Oh...ok, yeah it is. Felicia just showed me. It's Spock."

Giving a troll unsupervised access to Netflix Classics was a terrible idea. In this case, the draw was the original *Star Trek* tv shows. As the guys came into the yard through the side gate, they saw the aftermath: one troll, dressed in a perfect blue shirt with an embossed Enterprise logo and black pants. The explosive popularity of trolls had made troll-size clothing a booming business. Sure enough, he was hopping round the yard, chased by a loping and ungainly fifty-pound basset hound who could never quite decide if this was a small child or a very strange-looking rabbit. Either worked quite well for Clouseau.

Fortunately for Spock, Clouseau's attention shifted as the gate opened and he loped over to his people. That freed Spock to give the classic Vulcan hand sign. "Live long and prosper, boytoys!"

Sedrec was swamped with canine affection, leaving Ramon. "What brings you over here?"

"Nada. Linda's got *plans*. Too noisy! I figure here's better. Food?" Linda Alvarez tutored at the after-school program Ramon and his family had set up to help the poorer kids have a safe, healthy place to go. Her brother Cesar, Ramon's best friend as a kid, ran the place.

"Yeah, yeah. We're going to Zeffiro, and you can come."

"Pizza!"

The "butterfly effect" is when a tiny event triggers a subsequent chain of events.

The next few days were occupied by routine matters...after-action paperwork so they could collect a fee (or, more likely with the Feds, a tax credit), preparing a few potions (another contract), a trip to the vet for Clouseau. They hadn't been able to head over to the Las Cruces Youth Rec Center, their community support effort, until now. It was warming up; they loaded Clouseau and a large jug of water to cool him down with into the car.

On arrival, they saw and heard a small swarm of younger kids involved in some tag-like game, clearly led by Spock. Sedrec smiled; he was constantly amazed by how the trolls on Earth connected with human children. They all adored him. It wasn't just the look, although certainly that was a factor. No, they knew his other side and didn't fear it. And he could switch immediately to authority figure—he stopped the game momentarily to order one smiling young girl to sit down for a bit and drink some water.

The interruption was enough so all the kids saw the two men, and they waved hello enthusiastically as Clouseau bounded over to them. Off to the side, Ramon caught another girl walking in...Juanita Diaz, who was ten years old. He knew her because she had a magical gift that had surfaced quite recently.

"Hi, Juanita!" several voices chorused. "What took you so long? We thought you were coming with us from school."

FLAP.

"Huh? I did! What are you talking about? What time is it?"

That caught the men's attention, and Spock's. He moved to Juanita, sniffing and peering intently.

FLAP.

A low growl escaped. "Something is wrong here. Very wrong." He turned to the other kids. "Inside, please. Privacy."

Juanita was suddenly very scared. Sedrec pulled out his phone to call Juanita's parents as Ramon knelt. "It's ok, *mi linda*. We'll find out what's wrong, and I promise, we're gonna try to fix it."

Mr. Diaz was confused, afraid, and angry.

"So you're saying someone...or something...attacked my daughter to take her magic between school and here?"

"It looks that way. Trolls are particularly sensitive to magic, and Spock's never going to lie about anything that threatens any of the kids here. He says it feels like a tear in her magic; for what or how it happened, I don't know. It wasn't stolen altogether, fortunately. If it had been, she might not have gotten it back. It's kind of like a seedling right now; any damage may kill it.

"And no, neither of us has any idea how it could have been done or who did it, but I promise we are going to find out."

"And meantime?" He wasn't angry at Ramon; that was fear.

"It's a short walk for most of them, but it still happened. We'll talk to them, and I think I know some boys who will be willing to be escorts. Shouldn't take more than a day or two." He pulled a card from his wallet and wrote a few things on it. "I want you to take Juanita to Memorial and see this doctor. Have them do a complete physical; blood tests too. I'll call to set it up. Don't worry about the cost. It's on me. It's probably not needed, but better safe than sorry."

He knelt by the still-scared little girl. "Do me a favor, please. Don't do any magic at all, ok? I know it's fun, but... Just until we figure this out? Please?"

Meanwhile, Sedrec had been talking to Linda, Cesar, the other kids, and the doctor at Memorial who had some experience with magic. He waited until the Diaz family had left.

"Two other potential attacks. No one thought much of it. Spock can't tell; any marks are probably healed or fading with time."

"Any ideas on who or how?"

"Other than the obvious—that it was preparatory, not actual —no. That strongly says dark magic, but I can't take it further."

"Yeah, so I think we need to call in experts. Oh, and I promised we'd get escorts for the kids."

"Tuco's good. He'll tell his boys to keep the weapons hidden so the parents won't freak."

CHAPTER FIVE

School of Necessary Magic, Virginia

After breakfast the next morning, Sedrec opened a portal that deposited them at one of the designated arrival points near the School of Necessary Magic. As graduates and occasional guest speakers, the privacy wards recognized and ignored them. The Virginia morning saw few students out on the grounds; most were in class. Felicia, not surprisingly, immediately shifted and flitted off to gossip with the resident spirit and fairy populace. Sedrec's attention was drawn to one small cluster of girls talking animatedly some ways off.

"Well, that's not something you see every day." He pointed to the girls.

"Hmm? Oh... Ohh! A Drow?"

"Indeed. High lineage, too, I believe, judging by how the hair color is shifting."

"Wasn't there something on the grapevine about a bounty hunter and a Drow...out in LA, I think?"

"I believe so. Curious, in any case."

They walked into the main house and headed for the library. As they looked around the apparently empty room, a gnome busy in the stacks glanced over to see who was intruding so early in the day. Seeing the source, the red poppy on the brim of his bowler hat started blowing raspberries. Loudly.

"You two! You're not students anymore! I finally start sleeping soundly again without worrying about what you'll do next, and now? Shoo! *Shoo!*" Leo Decker was not a happy gnome, but that was nothing new.

"Aw, c'mon, Librarian Decker, we weren't *that* bad, were we?" Ramon's grin was impish.

"And we come bearing gifts." Sedrec held out a small bottle of Elvish Sunmead, an Oriceran cordial they knew the gnome enjoyed. "The matter that brings us here is rather less charming than Sunmead, though."

"Yeah, just a bit. There's something going on that's...not good, and we're not sure what it is. We're hoping you might know something.

"Hmph! Well. We'll see. Tell me what it is—and if you're wasting my time, you'll regret it!"

"Thanks, Librarian Decker! But not here. Too public."

The poppy stopped blowing raspberries at that. The librarian led them into a side room, casting an obscuration ward to block scrying.

Ramon recounted the information they had.

"And that's all we know right now. Any ideas?"

"Nasty business. Nasty. Not a creature. Creature would feed and the child would be dead, not this. No. Leeching magic, of a sort. Drow did that kind of thing. Atlanteans, too. For them, it was a form of torture. I've heard rumors that dark wizards sometimes did it to try to grow more powerful.

"This...I think it's close to that. Old magic. Blood magic. Setting up a link to draw off the child's magic. Early now, and small, so it's easy to hide, and no one will know. A child won't have a proper sense of its own power. And as the child grows, I suspect, the amount siphoned increases."

"So the mage is either using this to augment her own power or treating the kids like artifacts and recharging themselves from them. Something along those lines. Can we stop it, or block it somehow?" Ramon's hands, fidgeting with the scabbarded sword in his lap, betrayed his nerves and anger.

"Maybe, given time to study the effect."

"Time we cannot count on having before he or she retaliates." Sedrec's voice was icy.

"No. The hook is in place; assume the thief can choose to rip it out, if not use it to tap all the child's power at once. And, can the thief do this to one child at a time, or to all of them at once?"

"We don't want to find out."

The gnome nodded as he left the room.

"I don't see many options. Say we get the jump on them and knock them out. We still don't know that we can prevent them from snapping the taps given a free moment." Ramon's stomach churned.

"There's probably no bounty here. We won't have justification to act. We try to find proof that will hold before acting, but if we can't..."

"I'm not gonna let this escapee from the Malebolges kill my kids, Sed. No matter the cost."

CHAPTER SIX

Las Cruces, New Mexico

Nothing. Zilch. A big fat goose egg. That was the result of a week's worth of searching for clues about the predator in their town.

After returning from Virginia, they'd "hired" some of the boys who were part of Tuco Ruiz' crew. As magic had returned, diversion of law enforcement resources had left much of the rural Southwest open to increased gang activity. Many were satellites or channels for gangs in the larger cities like Phoenix, Vegas, and Los Angeles. Others had less savory connections, the Nuevo Gulf Cartel and the *Brujos Rojos* seeking to spread their influence. Tuco was a local, valley born and bred. He had ties, and ties meant commitments. Pulling on those, along with a judicious application of under-the-table cash for the boys, and the kids had discreet escorts when school let out.

That didn't address the issue of finding the dark mage or whatever it was. The bounty boards showed nothing, which wasn't surprising since the perp was apparently staying below the radar quite successfully. There were a few dark mages in the area, but none near the Holy Family/Pioneer Park area. An

Atlantean or Drow was possible but unlikely, at least in person. One could never rule out artifacts, and Atlantean devices fit the evidence on both the power and personality fronts.

Since they were drawing blanks anyway, Ramon decided to call a few connections in the tomb raiding business. It was a long shot, but...

"You want what again?"

All the agency reps followed the same script.

"Look, I know it's vague. I'm just checking on the possibility that someone found an unexpected artifact during a mission. One that wasn't turned in; whoever found it, kept it. Then they bugged out to keep the secret."

"Okay, so..."

"So maybe it was a raid gone bad, even if the target was recovered. Easier to keep a secret if you're the only witness or at least the only one in the area. It's possible the artifact caused a personality shift, so were there any sudden discipline problems soon after a raid? Or someone who bailed suddenly?"

"I can't discuss HR stuff. That's off the table. And you're probably still talking quite a few people."

"I'll take whatever leads you can give me. Oh, and you can probably limit things to people with at least minor magical abilities. What we're seeing suggests the artifact may augment magical power."

"That should help, but I can't promise anything."

And those were the *good* conversations.

The next few days were frustrating. The guys split their time between watching over the kids, checking (and rejecting) the infrequent responses from the tomb raiders, and casually walking through the nearby streets. They didn't figure it'd do any good, but it was better than nothing. Besides, Clouseau loved going for walks.

They had no expectations as they arrived at the Youth Center, nodding at Tuco as he made the rounds of his boys and making small (and smack) talk with Danny Alvarez, another of the kids identified as a target of the perp.

That was, until Danny stopped talking suddenly and started shaking.

"Yeah, you say that around Mr. Santos, and he'll smack ya a good one!" Ramon smiled as he said it, though. "And you'll have earned... Yo, Danny?"

"It's...her. I remember her now," Danny whispered.

Over there, off to the side, talking to a dazed Juanita Diaz. Ramon, Sedrec, and Felicia, who was on Sedrec's shoulder, all looked in that direction. Felicia *snarled* as she leapt down, shifting into wolverine form.

Unfortunately, the woman heard it and looked at the source. She didn't hesitate. Her hand darted to clutch Juanita's shoulder and she did...something...that made the girl scream and collapse.

The woman shifted, growing and twisting. Eight, then nine feet tall. Hideous. A thing from nightmares.

A hag.

"Danny, *run*! Tell everyone to stay away!" Ramon yelled as he and Sedrec erected shields. Just in time—the hag threw a blast of magic, but instead of being the green of rot and decay, this was laced with dark magic threads. The extra kick cracked Ramon's shield, the slimy goo splashing his left side. Ramon's head reeled from the light exposure.

Felicia leapt at the hag, her wolverine claws glistening with power, but the hag easily avoided her. Too bad; doing real damage would've been a bonus. Felicia had gotten between the hag and the child, though; taking care of this bitch wasn't her job. Sedrec repositioned a shield to cover both him and Ramon as he cut loose with a blast of light magic, only to see it casually absorbed by a mantle of dark power.

The hag's wild, maniacal laughter blasted out. "You are *insects*! You cannot stop me! They are mine! *Mine*!" She sent another blast at Ramon. This time, he used his blade as a channel to slice the spell. Sedrec's shield wavered but held. In return, the elf sent a shear wave through his blade, slashing high, trying to cut through the hag's black defenses. They held, also shakily.

The bitch was losing it. *How dare they!* She pulled out the amulet, clearly a dark magic artifact given its sinister pulsing blackness. She drew on it, rapidly creating another missile, hungry to consume magic and life and even soul. Both Ramon and Sedrec responded quickly. Ramon slashed it with another shearing wave, and Sedrec used a counter-missile. Ramon's wave disrupted the spell's structure even as it died, and Sedrec's blasted it apart.

"Breaching...now!" Ramon yelled as he focused a bright laser-like blast at the hag. It slammed into the amulet's protections and caused them to flare, seemingly without harming the hag.

But that wasn't the point. They'd developed this to crack defenses. The breach spell did just that—create a hole in an opponent's defenses and a channel for another spell to blast through the gap. Sedrec obliged with the Hammer, as they called the other half of the spell combination. The hag screamed in agony as several ribs were broken and dove desperately at Juanita, the dark magic from the amulet resembling a lamprey's mouth, open and ready to lock on. Felicia was there, however, and her claws slashed that hideous mouth, blocking it.

That gave Ramon and Sedrec time to repeat the Breach and Hammer with greater focus, purpose, and effect. Occupied as the dark amulet was, its shielding wasn't close to adequate. The hag's now-wide-open chest cavity sprayed the wall behind her with gore.

And even a hag couldn't regenerate from that much damage.

They both remained tense for a few moments in the aftermath, until Felicia hissed.

"Ah, sorry! You're right my dear! Sed, check her out. I'll go grab some potions."

Everyone was waiting for Mr. Diaz to arrive. Sedrec had given Juanita a healing potion and careful sips from an energy potion Ramon had brought back, along with Clouseau, who was busy licking Juanita's face. His tail was wagging furiously and making the girl laugh. Ramon's phone buzzed as a priority email came in. He checked it, then chuckled mirthlessly.

"Day late and a dollar short, guys."

He showed the message, which was from one of the tomb raiders, to Sedrec.

"Nice to have confirmation, but we've already dealt with one Clarita Ocaso."

FINIS

AUTHOR'S NOTES

There. I hope you like it. We're always hearing "write what you know" so that made the setting easy...I've lived here for thirty-plus years now, and I worked at White Sands Missile Range for several. My main goal was to get the three characters on paper, at least some. Ramon and Sed are largely modeled on Etheric Empire Rangers—freelance but cause-driven. Las Cruces and the surrounding area is their territory, because no one else is doing it. Felicia's just fun. Her concept's straight from gaming, specifically *Shadowrun*. I wanted her to be an entertaining but still very useful, sidekick. And Clouseau. Bassets are just the best. I still miss ours from when I was a kid. He's there to make me smile first and foremost, but I do hope he makes you smile too.

This was a lot of fun, and a fair bit of work. This isn't the type of coherent writing with which I have much practice. Tech writing, yes. Background writing for game worlds, yes...nothing published, just for personal use. And I have done a ton of gaming over the years, but that's more acting when you do it right than it is writing. I've got a process to develop should I want to do more of this. That may largely be up to you.

Again, thanks for reading, and thanks to Michael and Martha for Oriceran, and to the entire team at LMBPN for the opportunity.

Craig Lewis
Las Cruces, November 2018

OTHER SERIES IN THE ORICERAN UNIVERSE:

SCHOOL OF NECESSARY MAGIC
SCHOOL OF NECESSARY MAGIC: RAINE CAMPBELL
ALISON BROWNSTONE
THE DANIEL CODEX SERIES
THE LEIRA CHRONICLES
I FEAR NO EVIL
THE UNBELIEVABLE MR. BROWNSTONE
REWRITING JUSTICE
THE KACY CHRONICLES
MIDWEST MAGIC CHRONICLES
SOUL STONE MAGE
THE FAIRHAVEN CHRONICLES

OTHER BOOKS BY JUDITH BERENS

OTHER BOOKS BY MARTHA CARR

JOIN THE ORICERAN UNIVERSE FAN GROUP ON FACEBOOK!

BOOKS BY MICHAEL ANDERLE

For a complete list of books by Michael Anderle, please visit

www.lmbpn.com/ma-books/

All LMBPN Audiobooks are Available at Audible.com and iTunes. For a complete list of audiobooks visit:

www.lmbpn.com/audible

CONNECT WITH MICHAEL ANDERLE

Michael Anderle Social
  Website:
  http://kurtherianbooks.com/

Email List:
  http://kurtherianbooks.com/email-list/

Facebook Here:
  https://www.facebook.com/OriceranUniverse/
  https://www.facebook.com/TheKurtherianGambitBooks/

www.ingramcontent.com/pod-product-compliance
Lightning Source LLC
Chambersburg PA
CBHW050242110726
47898CB00007B/2241